PRAISE FOR MA

"A spokesman for those who were angry and beat, turbulent, temperamental and tortured ... In *The Graveyard*, Hłasko stabs his knife into the regime and draws it out dripping blood."

—*THE NEW YORK TIMES*

"Hłasko's story comes off the page at you like a pit bull."

—*THE WASHINGTON POST*

"Marek Hłasko lived through what he wrote and died of an overdose of solitude and not enough love." —JERZY KOSINSKI

"A self-taught writer with an uncanny gift for narrative and dialogue ... A born rebel and troublemaker of immense charm."

—ROMAN POLANSKI

"Hłasko writes with great talent ... Fascinates the reader with his conciseness, directness, and drama." —*SATURDAY REVIEW*

"As a study of a peculiar limbo, the endless wandering, the alienation, [*The Eighth Day of the Week* is] exquisitely drawn, and intensely young; it's about as good a description of being 18 as I've ever read, whether you're living under the yoke of communism or not."

—ZOE WILLIAMS, *THE GUARDIAN*,
"THE BOOK THAT CHANGED ME"

"While urging you to find and read ... any book by Marek Hłasko, I will yield to Hłasko's countryman, fellow writer, and friend Leopold Tyrmand, the final word: 'Even in his lies—and he was a man built of lies, some of them scurrilous, some of them charming—he conveyed always a truth. A truth we need.'" —JAMES SALLIS,
*THE BOSTON GLOBE*

# THE GRAVEYARD

**MAREK HŁASKO** (1934–1969) was born in Warsaw, the only child of parents who divorced when he was three. He was kicked out of high school and worked a series of menial jobs. While a truck driver, he began to write articles for a local newspaper, and soon after joined the crusading magazine *Po Prostu* as the editor of the literary section. In 1956, his short story collection *A First Step in the Clouds* won him immediate acclaim. It was followed by *The Eighth Day of the Week,* and two other novels, *The Graveyard* and *Next Stop—Paradise*. But when publishers refused to bring out his books, Hłasko traveled to Paris and published them in the émigré journal *Kultura*. It was a fateful decision: the Polish authorities gave him the choice of returning home and renouncing his work or staying abroad forever. He chose the latter, and spent the rest of his life in Western Europe, Israel, and the United States. He developed a reputation as a hard drinker and brawler, and was often in and out of prisons and psychiatric clinics. In 1966, Roman Polanski brought Hłasko to Hollywood to work as a screenwriter, but while there, he got into a fight with the composer Krzysztof Komeda, who died from his injuries a few days later. Six months afterward, Hłasko died from a fatal mixture of alcohol and sleeping pills. He was thirty-five years old and the author of ten novels, several collections of short stories and essays, and a memoir.

**NORBERT GUTERMAN** (1900–1984) also translated Hłasko's *The Eighth Day of the Week* and *Next Stop—Paradise*.

**JAMES SALLIS** is the author of *Drive* and the Lew Griffin series of crime novels, among many other books.

## THE NEVERSINK LIBRARY

*I was by no means the only reader of books on board the Neversink. Several other sailors were diligent readers, though their studies did not lie in the way of belles-lettres. Their favourite authors were such as you may find at the book-stalls around Fulton Market; they were slightly physiological in their nature. My book experiences on board of the frigate proved an example of a fact which every booklover must have experienced before me, namely, that though public libraries have an imposing air, and doubtless contain invaluable volumes, yet, somehow, the books that prove most agreeable, grateful, and companionable, are those we pick up by chance here and there; those which seem put into our hands by Providence; those which pretend to little, but abound in much.* —HERMAN MELVILLE, WHITE JACKET

# THE GRAVEYARD

---

# MAREK HŁASKO

TRANSLATED BY NORBERT GUTERMAN
INTRODUCTION BY JAMES SALLIS

MELVILLE HOUSE PUBLISHING
BROOKLYN · LONDON

THE GRAVEYARD

Originally published under the title
*Cmentarze* in *Kultura*, Maisons-Laffitte, 1956
First English publication in 1959 by William Heinemann Ltd.,
London, and E. P. Dutton & Co., Inc., New York
Translation copyright © 1959 by William Heinemann Ltd.,
London, and E. P. Dutton & Co., Inc., New York
Introduction copyright © 2013 by James Sallis

First Melville House printing: December 2013

Melville House Publishing        8 Blackstock Mews
    145 Plymouth Street     and   Islington
      Brooklyn, NY 11201           London N4 2BT

mhpbooks.com  facebook.com/mhpbooks  @melvillehouse

Library of Congress Cataloging-in-Publication Data

Hłasko, Marek.
    [Cmentarze. English]
    The graveyard / Marek Hłasko ; Translated from the Polish by
Norbert Guterman.
        pages    cm.
    Originally published under the title Cmentarze by E. P. Dutton
& Co., Inc., 1959.
    ISBN 978-1-61219-294-9 (pbk.)
    1. Psychological fiction.  2. Poland—Politics and government—
History—Fiction.  I. Guterman, Norbert, 1900–1984, translator.
II. Title.

PG7158.H55C613 2013
891.8'5373—dc23

                                        2013037462

Design by Christopher King

Printed in the United States of America
1  3  5  7  9  10  8  6  4  2

# INTRODUCTION

## BONEYARD SINGERS
### BY JAMES SALLIS

Forty years ago, while living in London, I was exposed daily, as editor and reviewer, to streams of literature in translation: Boris Vian novels, story collections from Central and South American writers, short-shorts and plays by Sławomir Mrożek, Penguin's *Writing Today* and Modern European Poets series. In the last I came across a volume dedicated to Zbigniew Herbert's work and, following it back to *Polish Writing Today*, recognized elements in contemporary Polish literature—a jaggedness and dislocation, a seepage of the absurd and alien into dailyness—that was very much to my taste. I think of these discoveries as a specific hunger: the tacit recognition of something, some essential nutrient, the individual needs.

Soon I was reading Tadeusz Różewicz (*I am twenty-four / led to slaughter / I survived*); learning about Aleksander Wat, to whom much later I would dedicate one of my poems; scouting out the early work of Jerzy Kosiński; curving my young spine over Czesław Miłosz; and sinking with great sighs and eurekas into the ever-amazing, encyclopedic work of Stanisław Lem.

And as any wanderer about the roads of modern Polish writing would, soon I happened upon Marek Hłasko.

Were this fiction, he would be leaning desultorily against a tree, smoking a cigarette with a noncommittal air, as I happened by. He would decline the ride I'd offer, saying that, at least for the moment, he isn't headed that way, but might I by any chance—his eyes at last meeting mine—spare a few złoty?

In 1965, situated for the moment back at Maisons-Laffitte, a town in the northwest suburbs of Paris where Jerzy Giedroyc, publisher of the émigré journal *Kultura*, had an office, Hłasko recalled his first stopover there upon his arrival in the West seven years before—before he spun, grasping for handholds, out into the world.

> In February 1958, I disembarked at Orly Airport from an airplane that had taken off in Warsaw. I had eight dollars on me. I was twenty-four years old. I was the author of a published volume of short stories and two books that had been refused publication. I was also the recipient of the Publishers' Prize, which I'd received a few weeks before my departure from Warsaw ... Disembarking from the plane at Orly Airport, I thought I'd be back in Warsaw in no more than a year. Today, I know I'll never return to Poland.*

Four years after writing those words, at age thirty-five and an exile for the past eleven years, Marek Hłasko was dead. He

---

* Quotations in this essay from Hłasko's memoir, *Beautiful Twentysomethings*, are taken from the Northern Illinois University Press edition (2013), translated by Ross Ufberg.

had overdosed on sleeping pills in Wiesbaden, Germany, on his way back to Israel from three years spent in the United States.

Paris, England, Spain, Germany, Switzerland, Austria, Denmark, the United States, Israel. One measures a circle beginning anywhere. So the spin, the circles of Hłasko's life, blurred watermarks on the well-used wood of a bar.

Marek Hłasko sprang into the spotlight, arms outstretched, with the publication of the story collection *A First Step into the Clouds* in 1956, followed fast by a novel, *The Eighth Day of the Week*. He had already gained fame for his short stories, for his literary and film criticism and, as editor, for turning the student weekly *Po prostu* into a national newspaper. Soon deemed Poland's most popular contemporary writer, in 1957 he was awarded the State Publishers' Literary Prize for the collection, while his novel put on the new skin of fifteen or more languages as well as an incarnation in film.

Then, within two years, Hłasko the darling, having brought out two novels abroad once Polish censors refused to pass them for publication, became Hłasko the despised.

"I was known as a finished man," he wrote in *Beautiful Twentysomethings*, the memoir quoted above, while ensconced again at the home of *Kultura*, which had brought out those two controversial novels, "and it was taken as a given, beyond any doubt, that I'd never write again. As I said, I was twenty-four years old. Those who'd buried me so quickly with the skill of career gravediggers were older than me by thirty years or more."

The brilliant young writer—onetime petty thief, onetime truck driver across treacherous mountain roads, onetime manual laborer and noncompliant spy on fellow workers, onetime journalist and editor, always a heavy drinker, always a mustang among saddle horses—becomes officially renegade. Attacked by the Polish press, and with permission to extend his visa refused, Hłasko makes the decision to remain abroad.

And so he wandered, so he spun out and sideways and back again. To Paris. To Switzerland. Giving interviews to the foreign press, cut off permanently from the world of Polish journalism and publishing. To West Germany. Working as a truck driver and manual laborer in Israel, where he wrote, in a two-year period, four extraordinary novels. To Spain and Denmark. Marrying, in 1962, Sonja Ziemann, who had played the leading role in the film version of *The Eighth Day of the Week*. Hanging with Polanski in Hollywood. Writing in 1969 his American novel, *The Rice Burners*.

Dying in Wiesbaden.

One of the novels that had been refused publication is the book you're holding now. Other early work largely ignored the established, Communist order; characters were outsiders chiefly because of their dogged insistence in pursuing their individual lives behind the wall. *The Graveyard* drove head-first into that wall. Thereafter, his characters would be not just outsiders but outcasts. With exile, Hłasko found his focus become at once tighter, in that he narrowed his observations to the fatally marginalized, the disavowed and dispossessed, and wider in that again and again he limned the question of how to live without faith, without belief. Agnieszka of *The Eighth Day of the Week* said it for them all: "The ideal is life without illusions." Hłasko wrote of the people among whom he had earlier lived and worked, and of those whom he, while subsisting on menial labor, stubborn determination, and his wits, had encountered at the places he'd touched down.

The road that led me to literature was very different
from the one followed by my fellow writers in Poland ... I came to it from below. And when I began to
write, I'd already seen so much that it was absolutely
impossible for me to believe in official truth.*

So, too, does violence push itself from the wings to center
stage, pulling behind it, as on a chain, all manner of inau-
thenticity, deception, and dissembling. In *Killing the Second
Dog*, a character looks "like an insect emerging into light for
the first time from under an overturned stone." One character declares: "My future? That's a word I won't be needing
anymore." Another: "There are no values left. That's why no
tragedy is possible today." And if no tragedy, then what? Characters impersonate the cartoon character Goofy, take on the
traits of movie types, spin duplicitous selves from spit, spite,
and thin air—filling the void with whatever comes to hand.

Often Hłasko himself seems to be much like his characters, barely clinging to the edge of the world, to the edge of
what he knows. Making his way not from streetlight to streetlight in the darkness but from stopgap to stopgap.

*The Graveyard* foreshadows much that was to come. The
novel skirts the border of and plunges into the sinkholes of
nihilism, a great zero burning at its heart: a circle around
nothing. Yet it goes about its business subversively. Its surface
bears up the simple tale of a man who loses all, a crooked
retelling, really—Job and the Great Collective—while, just
beneath, alligators glide and turn. Their eyes, their snouts are
visible for moments, then are gone.

---

* From a 1958 interview, translated by Thompson Bradley, with the
magazine *L'Express*.

All begins simply enough. Out for a visit with a friend, Franciszek Kowalski becomes a bit drunk and, singing an old patriotic song on the way home, is stopped and questioned by police, grows indignant, and gets jailed overnight.

"A party member," said the man in plain clothes, spreading his hands. "A former partisan, an officer, and—well? Just to look at you, Kowalski, one would say you're decent, quiet, probably a good comrade. But when we probe deeper, we find an enemy. You've unmasked yourself, Kowalski . . ." He gave the pile of papers a push. "That's the way it looks," he said. "You've unmasked yourself, and that's that."

His military service, his years of faithful, productive work, his countless hours of party meetings, his constant aid and counsel to fellow workers—none of this matters now, in light of that one evening. The first unmasking leads to another and, once set in motion, cannot be undone. As Archibald MacLeish wrote in *his* retelling of the Job story: "Saw it start to, saw it had to. / Saw it." Here, almost halfway through the novel, Kowalski goes for a walk along familiar streets.

From the dark streets the wind blew suddenly, picking up tatters of old posters and dragging them across the square. The second shift had begun; he could hear the roar of the engines, and the rattling and grinding of the machines. He passed the gate and walked out into the street; it ran far off into the darkness, and somewhere at the end of it drunks were staggering under the gas lamps, their shadows shrinking and crawling along the ground, or lengthening and sliding over the unlit windows of the houses. The sidewalk was wet and glassy. Franciszek looked down; in the puddles stars swam like fat worms.

People won't go without an idea, one of Franciszek's several confessors explains. Some new madman will always come along, grab hold of an icon, and run through the streets holding it aloft. The best revenge, he says, would be to create a new ideology. "To lead crowds to the sunny days of the future—that's the biggest joke of all."

A joke, or a lie? A question you well may ask yourself after reading *The Graveyard* and seeing what happens to poor, unsuspecting Franciszek Kowalski.

Friend and countryman Leopold Tyrmand said of Hłasko that he was "a man built of lies, some of them scurilous, some of them charming," setting the small lies of himself and his books against what he saw as a sea of untruth around him. Marek Hłasko lived and wrote in the interstice between what we see in the world and what we make of it, in that narrow crawlspace between outside and inside, self and world, where we all take up temporary habitation, never settlers, forever squatters.

One of us is a decent fellow—our public prosecutor; but to tell the truth, he is a pig too . . .

—GOGOL, DEAD SOULS

# THE GRAVEYARD

# I

FRANCISZEK KOWALSKI, FORTY-EIGHT YEARS OF age, slender, slightly balding, with a ruddy complexion, prominent cheekbones, and blue eyes, took a drink you won't believe how rarely, only on really extraordinary occasions; he never drank more than he could hold, and never had to be told later by others what he had talked about and how he had behaved. He was one of the lucky few who upon waking in the morning never have to be ashamed of the night before. Late one night, however, on his way home from a party meeting, a meeting which had dragged on for many hours, and at which he had often had to take the floor on matters of importance to him and his fellow workers, he ran into a friend whom he had known when they were both partisan fighters. He had not seen him since 1945 when he himself had marched off to the front while his friend, then seriously wounded, had gone to the hospital and stayed there until the end of the war. This meeting so delighted them that they decided to celebrate it with a glass of vodka. They went to the nearest bar. The friend ordered a half pint; and when the bottom of the bottle showed, Franciszek called the waiter, and, so as not to give his friend the impression that he had gone completely rusty since the days of the underground, ordered another half pint. This put them in such high spirits, they talked so heartily, and faded memories took on such brilliant colors, that they asked for a third half pint almost in one breath, and then the waiter himself, without asking them, served them a fourth. When they walked out, day was breaking, and the first bands of light were beginning to show in the gray sky. They said goodbye, affectionately shaking hands at great length, and then each went his way.

Franciszek walked briskly, keeping his eye on a line in the sidewalk, but he felt that some hitherto unknown forces were rocking him from side to side, and the line in the sidewalk kept vanishing from his field of vision. "I guess I'm a bit ..." he murmured, "a bit ... what the hell ..." And suddenly, to his own surprise, he began to sing in a tenor:

"O Polish woods, why do we love you so?
Because in your thickets we feel we're in heaven.
Under your wings
We aim our rifles safely at the foe ..."

Some men in overalls on their way to work laughed loudly and stared at him. This angered him so much that he too stopped.

"What the hell's the matter?" he cried. "You think I'm drunk or something?"

The others went by, but Franciszek kept shouting: "You think I'm drunk? Like hell I'm drunk! It's a lie. You're drunk yourselves ..."

Suddenly he saw two policemen before him. They were looking at him coolly and attentively. Franciszek wanted to say something, but he was still thinking of the workers who had offended him, and, instead of apologizing, cried once again, "You're the ones that are drunk!"

The policemen took a step toward him, and Franciszek, suddenly sobered, saw their faces close up. They were young, one a corporal, the other, with three stripes, a sergeant. The sergeant was very freckled and had a turned-up nose, and it seemed to Franciszek that his blue eyes held a cold threat as they looked at him from under the metal-edged visor of his cap.

"May we see your papers, Citizen?" asked the sergeant.

He extended his hand stiffly, and Franciszek stepped back.

"My papers?" he stammered out, taken by surprise. "What for?"

"Your papers, please," the sergeant repeated, and his voice sounded a little louder than before.

Franciszek put his hand in the pocket where he kept his wallet, but on touching the cold leather he stopped. "But—" he began.

Then the other policeman, who until then had been standing motionless and silent, alertly watching Franciszek's every move, thrust his face at him and cried: "Your papers. Do you understand? Or don't you?"

Franciszek drew out his wallet. He opened it with trembling hands, and gave his papers to the sergeant. The latter examined them, then pressed his leather bag against his knee and began to write something in a greasy little notebook with a black oilcloth cover.

"May I ask what you are writing?" Franciszek said, trying to look over the sergeant's arm.

The sergeant did not answer; he found it difficult to write in such an uncomfortable position, and Franciszek saw him knitting his brows and sticking out the tip of his tongue. After a moment he asked again: "Why are you taking down my name?"

"What's the matter, don't you like it?" the corporal asked sharply. "Maybe you don't like the police, Citizen?"

"I haven't said anything of the kind," Franciszek replied,

just as sharply. He looked at the corporal's chubby face, and
felt himself begin to shake with anger. By now the effects of
the liquor had entirely left him.

"You're not saying it now," the corporal said, and his childlike mouth twisted into a malicious smile. "Of course you're
not, now. But a moment ago you said the police were drunks."

"Who? Me?"

"No. Mrs. Malinowska."

"Come on, now. Don't take that attitude," Franciszek said
indignantly.

"Now it's our attitude you don't like. But a minute ago you
had the nerve to call us drunks." He looked at Franciszek with
superiority and said distinctly, "You're insulting the uniform,
Citizen."

"It's a lie!" Franciszek cried heatedly.

The corporal turned to the sergeant, who all this time had
calmly been writing in his black notebook. "Did you hear
that? This citizen says we're liars. Take that down."

Franciszek looked again at their young faces, and was
overcome with rage. Raising both arms, and shaking them
fiercely, he roared: "Take it down, you stinker, take it down!
And take down that you can stick it all up your ass, and that
I s— on everything . . ."

He was beside himself with fury. His own words came to
him as through a fog; he could neither understand nor distinguish them. He shouted incoherently, desperately waving
his arms. When his rage had passed, and he came to, he saw
that the sergeant was putting his identification papers into his
own leather bag.

"Let's go," the sergeant said dryly.

And, quite helpless, Kowalski went with them to the
nearby police station.

# II

THEY WALKED LESS THAN TEN MINUTES, AND
during that time Franciszek, whose strength had completely
evaporated after his fit of rage, gradually recovered his com-
posure. After a while he decided to put a good face on it,
and even began to whistle a tune. He assumed an attitude
of injured innocence. He held his head high, strode along
with assurance, and once, when he stumbled and noticed the
quick glance of one of the policemen, he smiled with ironic
superiority. When they entered the long dark passageway
leading to the police station, he thought: "There was no need
to fly off the handle. It was all because I was too tired and
drank too much. Vodka is really a gift of the devil. I'll never
get anywhere with these stupid kids. Maybe I really did make
an ass of myself. I must talk to someone sensible."

They crossed a small courtyard and entered a room where
there was a man on duty. Their entrance took no more than
a moment, but it made Franciszek feel ill at ease for the first
time since the incident in the street. First the younger policeman opened the door, then stepped back, and only after
Franciszek had entered did the two policemen follow, closing
the door behind them. The door made a particularly unpleasant squeak. "A fine state of affairs," Franciszek thought. "The
one place where things should run smoothly; they might
have oiled it. If only I could talk to someone sensible now."

He looked about him attentively, his face still impassive.
It was an unpretentious room, with walls of a nondescript

color, the room itself divided in two by a railing. Near the middle of the railing the paint which had once covered it was rubbed off; Franciszek thought that this must be because so many "customers" had leaned against it. On the walls hung portraits of government officials, and above them the Polish eagle. A wooden bench stood by one of the walls; a man was asleep on it, his back turned to the room. "You wouldn't say this place was very well run," Franciszek thought once again, and the thought gave him a kind of malicious satisfaction.

Meanwhile the policemen were behaving as though Franciszek did not exist. They were talking in an undertone with a man seated behind the railing. Franciszek heard his nasal voice but could not see his face, which was hidden by the backs of the policemen. For a minute or so he did not move, expecting to be asked to step up and make a statement, but nothing happened. Then, after listening awhile, Franciszek realized that they were not talking about him, but about a bicycle that had been reported stolen a week earlier. One of the policemen maintained that the thief was a certain Pasterka; the other, that the bicycle owner had sold it to pay for his drinks, and was afraid to admit it to his wife. "Damn the whole business," Franciszek thought. "If that's the way they're going to act, I'll tell them what I think of all this." He moved closer to the railing and saw that the policeman seated at the desk was also a mere corporal. This took him completely by surprise; he had thought that the men who had brought him here were talking with a lieutenant.

"I beg your pardon," he said loudly, moving to the middle of the room. "Could I speak to the chief?"

The policemen went on talking with the seated corporal for a while, then turned toward him.

"I'd like to speak to the chief," Franciszek repeated.

"Oh, yes," said the sergeant. He turned to the corporal at the desk. "I suppose we'll put this citizen in temporary. How are things in there today?"

"A bit crowded," said the man behind the desk. He cast a quick glance at Franciszek. "But there'll be plenty of room for him too."

"What temporary?" Franciszek asked.

"Take your things off," the sergeant said. He turned again, and Franciszek saw only his broad back crossed by a diagonal leather strap.

"What?" he asked.

"Didn't you hear me, Citizen? Take your things off, please. Your belt, scarf, shoelaces, and papers. And empty your pockets."

"We've given you the papers," said the corporal who had escorted Franciszek to the station.

"But why, damnit?" Franciszek asked.

The sergeant turned and looked at Franciszek with impatience. "What do you mean 'why'? You're under arrest," he said peremptorily. "Or do you think we've brought you here just to shake your noble hand?"

The three of them laughed uproariously. Franciszek was so startled that he did not even notice their laughter. "Under arrest?" he said. "What for?"

"Don't you know?"

"No," Franciszek said resolutely. He came close to the railing, and put his hands on it. "I do not know. I remember that I somehow flew off the handle, but it seems to me that's no good reason for keeping me locked up all night."

"No good reason?" the sergeant drawled. "And what about the things you shouted? Don't you remember what you shouted?"

The three of them stared at him, and Franciszek suddenly shriveled. For a moment they were all silent; the man asleep on the bench was breathing heavily.

"No," Franciszek said after a while. He passed his hand over his forehead. "I don't remember."

"Well, then, we'll talk after you've sobered up and can remember everything exactly," said the sergeant. "Then you'll sign a statement, and we'll let you go."

"Couldn't that be done now?" Franciszek asked.

The corporal at the desk laughed. "How can you make a statement," he inquired, "when you say yourself that you don't remember anything?"

"What do you mean? I remember everything."

"Everything?" asked the sergeant mockingly.

Franciszek's face fell. "Everything," he said in an uncertain voice, looking at the sergeant pleadingly. "Everything— except the exact words I shouted. I can't repeat them exactly, but if you remind me . . ." He made a vague gesture with his hand.

"We'll remind you in the morning," said the sergeant. "It's those words we're interested in. And now, that'll be enough, Citizen. Please hand us your belt, shoelaces, scarf, and everything you have in your pockets." He cast a reproachful glance at Franciszek, and added gently, "Don't make it hard for us, Citizen."

"But—" Franciszek began.

The corporal behind the railing banged his fist on the desk. "Do you or do you not understand human speech? Hand over your things, and don't talk so much, or you'll be sorry!"

With trembling hands Franciszek began to remove his things from his pockets and put them on the desk—a handkerchief, a comb, a little mirror, a fountain pen, and a pencil. The corporal made a list of them and thrust them into an enormous gray envelope; on it he wrote in clumsy letters, "Franciszek Kowalski, 3.28.1952." He went to a cupboard and opened it. Out of the corner of his eye Franciszek noticed that there were many such envelopes, placed evenly one beside another, indistinguishable. The corporal closed the cupboard and sat down again at the desk. He handed Franciszek a receipt and, pointing to the place with his finger, said dryly, "Sign here."

Franciszek signed and gave him back the paper. "I am a former partisan," he said bitterly. "Never in my life have I done anything I could be ashamed of." His words came out with increasing speed. "Someone will pay for this mistake. It's unheard-of that a man should be locked up just for taking a few glasses of vodka. You must believe me; this is the first time in my life I have ever been in a police station."

"That's fine," the corporal said without even looking at him. "But there is a first time for everything."

The sergeant said, "And now, please, follow me."

Holding up his trousers, Franciszek followed him. They walked along a filthy dark corridor lit only by small wire-encased bulbs hung near the ceiling. Then the sergeant opened a door, and said, "Here."

Franciszek walked in; he wanted to say something, but at that moment the door banged shut. He stood still for a moment, listening; his thoughts could not catch up with the pace of events. He leaned his hand against the wall, and withdrew it in disgust: the wall was rough, cold, and clammy. The sergeant's footsteps died away.

# III

UNTIL THE MOMENT WHEN HE HEARD THE DOOR bang shut, Franciszek had not clearly realized his position: everything had happened too quickly, in an atmosphere of hysteria that didn't seem quite real. Not until he had been in the stuffy cell for a while, and his eyes had become sufficiently accustomed to the half darkness to distinguish the people lying on the floor, did he realize that he would irrevocably remain a prisoner for several hours. At first this realization threw him into a rage, and he pounded and kicked the door; but, as no one responded, he soon grew tired; a little later he was even amused. "The whole thing is ridiculous," he thought. "Nothing but a stupid mistake; somebody will have to pay for it later."

Calming down, he examined the cell. Around him, on the floor and on the two benches, people were sleeping. They seemed shriveled, comically small. They slept in all sorts of positions, strangely doubled over, with legs pulled up to their chins; and a giant of a man, whose bald head gleamed faintly in the dim light, slept standing, his hands clinging to an iron netting on the wall. Franciszek tried to sit down on the floor; but as he squatted he suddenly felt a pair of legs being pulled from under him, and someone said hoarsely, "Watch what you're doing, damn you!"

Franciszek got up, and once again took two uncertain

steps, trampling on arms and legs; their owners jerked them back with sudden froglike motions. The air was heavy with the smell of stale alcohol; even now, when they were asleep, their mouths drooling, it was obvious that almost everyone in the cell was dead drunk. "At least, this is my first time," Franciszek thought, and the reflection comforted him. "After all, one out of every five men is always drunk. It must be discouraging for the police. I was a bit tight, I made too much noise, and that was the cause of all the trouble. Nothing to be upset about. Come on, pull yourself together. You're getting to be a nervous wreck; you're petering out, and it's all because you're tired. You shouldn't have drunk all that vodka; that's why you behaved like a bum in the street. I suppose all of us have to play hooky every now and then, no matter how old we are." At that moment he felt almost grateful to the police for having brought him here, to this dark cell, filled to the last inch with drunks, thereby teaching him a bitter lesson. "Yes, you stupid old bum, this will teach you," he thought, clenching his fists with rage.

At last he found a bit of free space, and sat down on the cold concrete, resting his chin on his knees. "You've got what you deserve, you fool," he said to himself. "You could have slept in a comfortable bed, under a warm blanket; you could have had a glass of tea with lemon, and you have only your own stupidity to thank, old man, for having to spend the night curled up like an embryo. You'll be a fine-looking mess when they come to let you out."

Someone beside him suddenly wakened, sat up with a groan, yawned widely, and began to rub his eyes, all the while grumbling like a bear. Then he turned an indistinct face toward Franciszek. "Captain, do you happen to have a cigarette?" he asked.

Franciszek automatically patted his pockets. "No," he said; "they were taken from me."

The other man moved closer. "What for?" he asked hoarsely.

"What do you mean, what for?"

"Why did they arrest you?"

"Oh," said Franciszek, smiling. "I was a little tight, that's all. I just sang in the street."

After a moment of silence, Franciszek's neighbor said in a worried voice: "That's bad. Very bad."

"Bad?" Franciszek asked. "Why?"

"You can get a long term for singing," the other said. "You think it's only a song, nothing at all; you think you're innocent, still . . . Did you resist?"

"No, not at all; I only flew off the handle a bit."

The stranger yawned. "Knock on the door," he said. "If someone comes, ask him; maybe they'll let you go. What time do you think it is?"

"I don't know. Three, maybe later . . ."

The stranger pondered awhile. "By now Lieutenant Malinowski should be on duty," he said. "He's a good egg. If he comes here, ask him politely, and he'll let you go—if it's true you didn't do anything."

"But of course I didn't do anything," Franciszek said with a shrug. "I'm telling you, I was a little drunk, and I sang."

"What did you sing?"

"Does it matter?"

"Of course it does. There's a world of difference between one song and another. What did you sing about?"

"I don't remember, and then, it's really beside the point . . . An old army song."

The stranger whistled. "Couldn't be worse," he said. "You're in for it, sure as the Our Father ends with Amen." He bent over someone, and shook him by the arm. "Mr. Sikorski, Mr. Sikorski! Would you sing the song they locked you up for?"

A man invisible in the darkness sang:

"Once I walked home late at night
And suddenly it's the end of my freedom.
Plain-clothes men, tommy guns,
Identification, secret po-o-o-lice . . ."

The singer finished, and swore lustily. Franciszek's neighbor said: "Now, you see. There's a difference between one song and another. If you were singing that when they hooked you, it would be bad."

"I've never heard it before," Franciszek said. "And I'd never sing anything so stupid. I'm telling you, I sang an old army song."

"You must remember what it was," the other said resolutely. "It's vital. You have to know why they locked you up. When you're questioned you have to know what it's all about, and how to behave. What song could it be? 'The Legions'? Probably not, or you'd remember. Anyway, 'The Legions' doesn't amount to a hill of beans; at the most you'd get eighteen months for it. What damn' thing can it be? Aha," he drawled, "could it be this? Just a moment." He shook someone violently. The shaken man sat up and began to rub his eyes. Franciszek's neighbor asked: "Mr. Nowak, what were you singing when they picked you up?"

The man addressed as Mr. Nowak sobbed a moment, and then sang in a gentle, soft tenor:

16 MAREK HŁASKO

"Great Marshal Stalin, long live he!
His lips are sweet as raspberry!
He is my dream, for him I long,
He is my life's enchanting song."

No sooner had he finished than he lay down to sleep again. Franciszek's neighbor asked: "Was that it?"

"No."

"Please, try to remember. Sometimes you get more for a joke than for a song." He suddenly turned around and called out into the darkness, "Hey, Mr. Aleksandrowicz!"

"Yes," someone said at the other corner of the cell.

"What did that fellow get, the one that was here last month—you know, the one that told the joke about Little Boy Joe?"

"His case hasn't come up yet," came the reply from the other corner, "but I don't think he'll get off with less than five years. The other fellow who was with him and told the grain-hoarding joke got three years, so how much would you think the other one's good for?"

Franciszek's neighbor sighed. "You see," he said, "there are words and words. Well, brace yourself ... Happen to have a cigarette?"

"I told you I didn't," Franciszek said. The conversation was getting on his nerves.

The stranger yawned. "Too bad," he said. "You won't mind, then, will you, if I take a litle nap to get my strength back. Every time I spend the night here I dream of grapevines in the southern sunlight. I love Greece. I have visions of noble-faced sages in long tunics, of virgins in transparent robes gliding about among cypresses in full bloom. Even in this cell I can hear their songs throbbing with the joy of life ..."

Leaving the sentence unfinished, he dropped like a log, and began to snore with such force that Franciszek shuddered.

Once again Franciszek had a fit of rage. "Damn it," he thought, "is it really fair that just because a man sings out loud in the street he should be locked up for the night with hooligans and drunks? Just because a man takes a glass of vodka, must he be treated like the lowest kind of tramp?"

He stood up abruptly, and, heedless of the groans and growls of those he was trampling on, walked to the door and pounded it until his fists hurt. No one came; he could hear only screams and curses, coming probably from another cell at the end of the corridor. Franciszek kicked the door, once, twice; only then did he hear the clicking of a lock somewhere far away, followed by the sound of footsteps. "At last," he thought, relieved, and wiped his forehead. The lock creaked, the door opened slowly, and before him stood a small man with a jolly round face, wearing the uniform of a lieutenant. "This must be the one," Franciszek thought with satisfaction; "this must be the lieutenant that fellow talked about."

"What do you want?" the lieutenant asked. His voice was calm and soft, with none of that irritating coldness that characterizes bureaucrats the world over, and Franciszek felt at once that he could trust him.

"I'd like to talk with you," he said, trying to speak politely and distinctly.

"What do you want?" the lieutenant repeated.

"I have the impression that I was arrested by mistake. I was only walking in the street; I might have been a little tight, and I don't know why I felt like singing; after all, I'm no kid, and I was once shot in the lungs, and I'd like to avoid catching cold. Could you release me?"

The lieutenant scrutinized him awhile. "Hold out your

arms and close your eyes," he said. He said it very courteously, and Franciszek complied at once. "And now," said the lieutenant, "tell me quickly your name, address, and occupation."

"My name is Kowalski; I live in the Muranów housing project; I work in an automobile repair factory as assistant technical director."

"Fine," said the lieutenant. "Drop your arms. I'll see what I can do."

Opening his eyes, Franciszek saw that the lieutenant was smiling. "Come with me," he said. He closed the door; once again they walked along the stinking dimly lit corridor. The whole police station reeked of stale alcohol; the stench was so strong that Franciszek was disgusted with himself.

"How did you get shot in your lungs?" the lieutenant asked.

"In the underground," Franciszek said. "In 1943."

"You were a partisan fighter?"

"Yes."

"The National underground or the Communist underground?"

"The Communist. The People's Army."

The lieutenant smiled again. "And now you've gone and got yourself arrested," he said.

Franciszek perceived a note of friendly chiding in his voice. "Those boys of yours are so serious," he said, "I couldn't talk them out of it."

"What can we do?" the lieutenant replied. "This is your first time. Occasionally people have too much fun, and our job is to keep order in the streets."

They walked on a bit and found themselves in a small empty room. The lieutenant said: "Wait here a minute. We'll release you shortly."

Franciszek sat down on the bench and luxuriously stretched his numbed legs. "At last," he thought. "Here is a sensible fellow that can listen to reason. The fact is, I'd have been home by now if I hadn't been so damn touchy. It's a good thing I told Elzbieta about this meeting; she won't be worried. It looks as though there's something to say for meetings, though you'd never think so in advance. A bit of vodka, exhaustion, nerves—that's all it takes to find yourself in a cell. Oh, to hell with it!"

The door opened, and the lieutenant came in. Franciszek looked at him with a smile, and then was dumfounded: it was as though an entirely different man was standing before him. During those few minutes the lieutenant's friendly young face had managed to assume the repellent mask of officialdom and contempt. He looked at Franciszek with cold, venomous eyes. "We're going back," he said dryly.

Franciszek rose. "Where to?"

"The cell."

"But why?"

"You're under arrest," the lieutenant said. He stared at Franciszek as if he were an inanimate object; a note of impatience had crept into his voice. "Haven't you had time to realize that, Kowalski?"

"But why? What for? I did nothing wrong. Can't you at least tell me what for?"

"You'll know in due time," said the lieutenant. He pointed to the door. "If you please."

"I've got to know right away," Franciszek cried. "I won't go anywhere until I know."

The lieutenant walked up to him, put his hand on his arm, and leaned toward him. Franciszek shriveled, suddenly seized with fear.

"The fact that you're a party member and former partisan makes no difference now," he said. "The only thing that matters to us is that you are a man we must hold. No use thinking about the other things; I'm afraid they don't matter. And now, let's go." He pressed Franciszek's arm with his unexpectedly powerful fingers. Franciszek rose and followed the lieutenant. He did not say a word as they walked along the corridor. The lieutenant too was silent, walking erect, his legs stiff as though he were on parade.

Back in his cell, Franciszek sat down again on the bit of concrete from which he had arisen a few minutes earlier to set out on his futile journey. "What's going on?" he thought feverishly. "For God's sake, what do they want of me?"

The man at his side stirred and once again sat up rubbing his eyes like an ape. "Have you brought some cigarettes?" he asked after a long, powerful yawn.

Franciszek shook with rage. "Stop bothering me—you and your cigarettes," he growled.

The stranger smiled. "That's the way it is," he said. "They're in no hurry. If they want to, they can keep you here so long you'll never want to laugh again."

"What could I have done?" Franciszek asked, speaking to himself rather than to his neighbor. "What in the world could I have done? I keep trying to recall every word I said, everything that happened, and I can't understand a thing. If only they would tell me, but they won't. What could I have done?"

The stranger stretched luxuriously. "Each one of us imagines he didn't do anything," he said. "Each one of us somehow thinks he is innocent. But then a moment comes when others begin to have power over him, and then our thoughts don't matter, and only what they think about us matters." He sighed and turned over. "Thank God I'm nothing but a drunk," he said. "That's the only thing that gives me some sort of assurance; if anyone thinks anything about me, it will be only that. Good night. Try to get some sleep. And pretend the whole thing is a dream. A rotten, stupid dream, from which we'll never awaken."

# IV

AT LAST DAYBREAK CAME, AND WITH IT A PIERCING
cold invaded the cell. Gray light filled the little window up
by the ceiling. The faces of the recumbent men became more
distinct, emerging from the darkness, puffy, disheveled, with
bloodshot eyes. One after another, they sat up on the concrete floor; they looked about them unseeing, then, yawning
and shivering, rose on shaky legs. From the street came the
first sounds of the awakened city—passing trucks, hurrying
footsteps, creaking tramcars.

Franciszek had sat numb while the cell was dark and silent; his only emotions had been anxiety and anger. But now
the realization that only a few yards away, just outside the
police station, hundreds of thousands of people were living
a normal life without his being able to share in it threw him
into a fit of dejection such as he had not experienced for a
long time. "This is perhaps the worst thing that can happen
to a man," he thought. "Worse than sickness, solitude, any
kind of misfortune. To be cut off from the life of others—can
there be anything worse? Is there anything that can get you
further down? I've had only a few hours of this; how terrible
must be the life of a man condemned to endure it for long!"
He was seized by only one overwhelming desire: to get out as
soon as possible, to be in the streets, in the midst of people
and the city bustle.

The door creaked. The lieutenant appeared in the doorway. A card in his hand, he said: "Romanowski, Bolder, Krupinski, come out."

Three men rushed to the door. Franciszek followed them. "And what about me?" he asked.

"Wait," said the lieutenant.

"I could still get to my job on time," Franciszek said.

The lieutenant shut the door in his face without answering; Franciszek had barely time to jump back. Several of his cellmates laughed. "You'll pay for this," he thought resentfully. "You'll pay for all your stupidities. I'll see to it that all of you are thrown off the force, straight out on your faces. That'll show you that you can't treat an honest citizen like this." Pacing back and forth, he planned all kinds of vengeance for everything they had done to him here.

The cell grew animated; the inmates recalled the events of the day before. Some cracked jokes; others sat staring vacantly. One man kept saying: "What am I going to tell my wife? What am I going to tell my wife? I promised her this would never happen again."

On one of the benches three young men were sleeping. The others felt sorry for them, seeing them huddled together like kittens. All of them wore homemade clothes, narrow trousers, yellow shirts, and garish socks. Their faces were black and blue, and their noses were smashed; they had obviously been arrested for brawling.

Suddenly one of them woke up. He ran his fingers through his hair, and nudged his companions. "Kusiatynszczak, get up!" he cried. "The sun is up. Time to go to work."

The other two awoke. They exchanged affectionate glances, then sang in hoarse voices:

"Welcome you comrades, to work, to work,
Our factories bustle, our furnaces blaze,
My country, my home, my happy home,
To build a house of dreams by our common efforts . . ."

"Shut up," someone growled. Franciszek looked at him: he was the giant with the bald head who had slept standing up.

The door creaked again, and all glanced toward it. In the doorway stood the lieutenant and a man in civilian clothes. The latter was small; he had a surprisingly round face, a thin nose, and dark eyes set very close together.

"Kowalski," the lieutenant said. "Will you come here, please."

Franciszek walked to the door and stood facing the man in plain clothes. The other looked him over. Franciszek caught only a glimpse of his eyes, but it seemed to him that his innermost thoughts were being read.

The man in plain clothes turned to the lieutenant. "Is this the one?" he asked.

"Yes," said the lieutenant.

"Citizen Lieutenant," Franciszek said quickly, "please hurry up, I'd like to—"

"Let's go," said the man in plain clothes.

They banged the door right in his face, and once again he barely had time to jump back. The stranger with whom Franciszek had talked during the night let out a soft whistle. "So that's what it is," he said.

Franciszek turned to him. "What do you mean—'that's what it is'?"

His neighbor looked at him with gentle irony. "You must have made a fine mess for them to come after you like that," he said. He smacked his tongue in a particularly repulsive way, then went on: "If you don't remember what happened, you're surely in for it. Someone must have informed on you. Don't you remember?"

Franciszek looked at him sharply. "What are you talking about?"

The stranger smiled. "Someone must have informed on you," he repeated. "Maybe you listen to Free Europe. You'd be in a bad way if it turned out that you listen to those broadcasts and then tell other people what you've heard. We've got one of those in here; he can tell you." He called over his shoulder: "Mr. Kwiatuszynski, would you kindly come here for a minute?"

The bald-headed giant came up to them. "I'm listening," he said in a splendid bass.

Franciszek's neighbor turned to him. "You're here because of Free Europe, aren't you?"

"Nothing of the kind," the giant said with great dignity. "I never listened to Free Europe. I was locked up for listening to Radio Madrid. My wife turned it on full blast, and the woman next door informed on us. It goes to show, you can never trust a woman."

"It doesn't matter," Franciszek's neighbor said, smiling triumphantly. "What matters is the fact itself, not the details. And Madrid is probably worse in this respect . . ."

"That's not true," said someone in the rear of the cell. "The worst is New York. *They* really hate us."

"The Vatican is just as bad," someone else threw in, coming closer. He was a small gray-haired man who looked like a retired teacher. "You'd think they'd apply different standards to a purely religious program, but nothing of the kind. The trouble my stepson got into for repeating a Vatican announcement—well, I wouldn't wish it on anyone else. The name of a broadcasting station doesn't prove anything. In such cases, my friends, everything is an illusion—"

Franciszek's neighbor interrupted the argument with an impatient wave of his hand. "There's no need to go into all that," he said. "The main thing is that this gentleman here"— he pointed to Franciszek—"has been informed on, and he has absolutely no idea who it can be." He leaned close to Franciszek's ear. "Somebody in your family? You think the family is so wonderful? Well, we have somebody here because his mother-in-law reported he had a gun. She did it out of spite, because he didn't ask her to his birthday party."

"He isn't here any longer," the giant said in his splendid bass. "He was released yesterday."

Franciszek cast a sharp glance at his neighbor. "Stop bothering me," he said. "You offend me as a man and as a party member. I am honest, and the fact that I am here with you is just an unfortunate mistake. Please don't talk to me like that, or I'll tell the officer on duty what I think of you."

His neighbor looked at him attentively. "What do you want of me?" he asked, shrugging his shoulders. "I haven't said anything."

Franciszek's nerves, strained to the breaking point, this time refused to be controlled. He began to scream, his mouth foaming, his arms waving hysterically. "You haven't said anything? All this time you've been saying the most disgusting things! Who do you think you're talking to? I am a former partisan, and I didn't fight through the whole occupation to hear people like you sneer at everything. I made a hash of people like you with my own hands in the underground. You offend everything I believe in and our country believes in! Do you understand?"

The man looked at him coldly. "I never said anything to

you," he said. "Do you hear me? I didn't speak to you. It's you who have been bothering me."

"I? I bothered you?" Franciszek choked.

The man turned to the others. "Have I said anything to this gentleman?" he asked very loudly and calmly.

There was a moment's silence, then the bald-headed giant said softly to Franciszek, "The gentleman said nothing."

"What do you mean?" Franciszek was indignant. He was trembling, and beads of sweat appeared on his forehead. "Didn't he drivel about denunciations, and so on?"

"You're raving," said the bald man, and gave Franciszek a light push on the chest. "Everything's got mixed up in your head, my friend. I myself heard you say you'd like to make a dash for the West, that you'd be better off there. Do you remember that or don't you? Everybody here heard you say it!"

"Who did?" Franciszek cried. He turned violently to the others. "Who heard me say that?"

For a moment there was complete silence. Franciszek breathed heavily. He felt the sweat streaming down his body, causing an intolerable itch.

"All of us," the cell replied.

The bald man added: "And don't you try to bother anyone. You were very drunk, and you don't remember what you said last night. If I were to repeat it, you'd be in serious trouble. If you know what's good for you, keep quiet."

Franciszek stepped back. Hatred cast a mist over his eyes; he crouched, ready to spring at the bald giant, but at that moment the door creaked again, and Franciszek automatically turned his head.

"Kowalski," the lieutenant said. "Come along."

He was led down the corridor, to the room where he had

been taken the previous night. Now, in daylight, it looked even grayer and uglier than before, when it was lighted by a bright, unshaded bulb hanging in the middle of the ceiling. At the desk the corporal's seat was occupied by the round-faced man in plain clothes. Next to him was the sergeant who had escorted him to the police station. He looked very tired; his young face was pale, and he had rings under his eyes. The three of them—the lieutenant, the man in plain clothes, and the sergeant—were unshaven; during the night the sergeant's round cheeks had grown as downy as ripe peaches, and neither his uniform nor his heavy gun added to his dignity.

The man in civilian clothes raised his eyes from the papers spread on the desk. "Well, Kowalski, here you are." His voice expressed sincere worry. "It looks bad for you."

Franciszek was silent; frowning, he leaned against the railing, and looked at the man in plain clothes.

"Bad," the other repeated. Then, shaking his head, "You're really in hot water."

"What the devil have I done?" Franciszek asked.

"What's the matter, aren't you satisfied?" the lieutenant asked. Pushing out his chin, he stared at Franciszek with the expression of a little boy getting ready to fight.

"I want to know what I have done," Franciszek said.

"And I want you to tell me," the lieutenant said, "whether you like it or not."

"Yes," the sergeant threw in, "tell us: Don't you like it? What? Do you like it or don't you?"

"A party member," said the man in plain clothes, spreading his hands. "A former partisan, an officer, and—well? Just to look at you, Kowalski, one would say you're decent, quiet, probably a good comrade. But when we probe deeper, we find an enemy. You've unmasked yourself, Kowalski ..." He gave the pile of papers a push. "That's the way it looks," he said. "You've unmasked yourself, and that's that."

"Me?" Franciszek stammered. "Unmasked myself? What *is* this all about?"

"Maybe you don't like it here," the sergeant said. "Tell us: Don't you like the regime? Or maybe the police?"

The man in plain clothes rose from his seat. His legs wide apart, he looked straight into Franciszek's eyes. "You have insulted the party," he said calmly. "You have insulted the uniform of the People's police. You have insulted the People's Poland. You abused the party and the People's government in such language that I'm ashamed to repeat it. All this was taken down verbatim. Do you remember that? You, a party member, as your papers show, you have insulted our government, our People's regime. By this token you have shown what you really are, *Mister* Kowalski. Be good enough to read this, and sign it, *Mister* Kowalski. Then you'll pay the fine and you'll go home. We'll inform the secretary of the party organization. We'll send him a copy of the record. And now— please." He handed Franciszek a sheet of paper and a pen.

"My God," Franciszek stammered, "is it possible?" His knees were trembling, and his heart was pounding somewhere in his throat.

"Pretend that it is," the lieutenant said. He cast a glance at Franciszek, who was as pale as a sheet, and grinned crookedly. "Stop play-acting," he said sharply. "You think one thing and you say another. We're not here to be taken in by such tricks. One day you shout obscenities in the streets; the next day you'll be a spy. Read this, please, and sign."

"But I couldn't possibly have shouted like that!" Franciszek cried. "There's some mistake. I refuse to believe that I said such things."

"I heard you," the sergeant said. "And if you don't like it, just say so."

"I don't think that way."

"You shouted that way," said the man in plain clothes. "These are your words. I am ashamed to repeat them, party comrade."

"What a sober man thinks in his heart a drunk says with his tongue," the lieutenant said. "Surely no one knows that better than you."

"A mistake," Franciszek said hoarsely. He raised his hand to his forehead as though he were going blind. "A mistake."

"That's right," said the man in plain clothes. "You made a mistake. You made a mistake if you thought the enemy can never be unmasked."

Franciszek glanced at the paper he had been handed. He tried to read it, but the letters blurred before his eyes into a single formless mass. Suddenly he had the feeling that everything around him was unreal, make-believe. He closed his eyes; on opening them after a moment, he saw the lieutenant bending over him. A little farther off stood the man in plain clothes, and next to him, the sergeant. Their faces showed nothing but contempt.

"Here," the lieutenant said, pointing to the place where he had to sign.

"I—" Franciszek began. He stopped suddenly. He realized that he was at the end of his rope, and that he would not be able to say a word to justify himself before these men. In the corridor someone was banging his fists on the door, roaring, "Let me out! Let me out!" Franciszek thought: "I've got to get out of here, get out at any cost." He picked up the pen, and signed. The lieutenant took the paper from his hands and threw it on the desk.

Later, as they returned his things, he could see the police-men talking to him, but their words were no more distinct than the buzzing of a fly. A void opened within him, and he could not find a single thought to fill it with; he put on his necktie, laced his shoes, and buckled his belt, moving like a sleepwalker. Not until the lieutenant had opened the door did he hear the man in plain clothes say to him, "So long, *Mister* Kowalski."

And he found himself in the street.

# V

THE ICY WIND BLOWING FROM THE VISTULA
revived him a little; the day was misty and cold, and the pale
sun glistening feebly on the damp roofs carried not a hint of
spring; no one would have suspected that the sap was already
gathering under the bare branches of the trees. He walked
fast, straight ahead, his crumpled overcoat unbuttoned; he
had no idea where he was going; he was filled with only one
desire—to get as far away as possible from the scene of his
nocturnal ordeal. "The whole thing is a stupid accident," he
muttered to himself. "It's perfectly insane. Everything will be
cleared up soon; damn it all, it must be cleared up! I'll settle
the matter right away; I'll go to see whatever person I have
to ..." He caught the amused glances of the passers-by, and
realized that he had been talking to himself; he buttoned his
overcoat and slowed his pace.

In the window of a little shop he saw a sign, TELEPHONE.
He pushed the door open and entered; the shop bell above
the door tinkled shrilly. Out of the darkness came the smell
of stale vegetables. A young girl was standing at the telephone; Franciszek moved aside.

"What can I do for you," asked the proprietor, unshaven,
in a dirty smock.

Franciszek pointed to the girl: "I want to use the phone..."

The proprietor gave a grunt of disappointment, and
buried his dark face in the newspaper. "We Are Advancing

Toward ..." a headline screamed. After a moment he turned the page. "Yesterday's speech caused wide repercussions ..." The girl was chirping into the receiver, her lips curving deliciously: "Dzidka? Impossible! Is that so? ... It's true, she always ... I don't want to say anything mean about her, but it's only what you'd expect ..."

The bell above the door tinkled. Franciszek shuddered as though touched by an electric current. A boy came in; his sharp eyes glinted under the visor of his cap. He put a jar on the counter. "Milk and half a pound of butter."

"... Dzidka? With Romek? Yes, I always ..."

"There's no milk. I have potatoes."

"... I've always said ..."

"And the butter?"

"No butter. I'll have Brussels sprouts this afternoon."

"I'll telephone, and the whole thing will be cleared up," Franciszek thought. He looked resentfully at the girl's little painted mouth. "I'll telephone; I'll go to the factory, and everything will be settled."

"And lard?"

"No lard, but I have potatoes."

"... I've always said to Stefan, 'Look out, you can never tell what she might do' ..."

"When will you have butter?"

"How the devil do I know? I told you what there is. Now get out!"

The bell tinkled again, startling Franciszek; the boy walked out. He ran across the street, splashing through a puddle; his shoes were at least three sizes too big for him. "Fool," thought Franciszek in irritation; "some day he'll break his leg." He glanced at his watch: he was already an hour late; he must telephone ...

"... you know me, you know I never say bad things about
my girl friends; but in this case ... What? It isn't Dzidka?
I know it isn't Dzidka, of course not. But to get back to
Wladka..."

He put his hand on her shoulder; she turned around.
"Three minutes," he snapped. "Enough."

"Can't you be polite?"

"Can't you grow up?"

She flung some coins on the counter, and, looking at him
with rage, walked out, slamming the door; once again the
bell tinkled at the very center of his tired brain. The worn dial
swung in its arc like a pendulum. "The Be-Kind-to-Animals
Veterinary Home," said a voice in the receiver. "Sorry, wrong
number," he muttered. In the end he managed to dial the right
number; there was a continuous ringing—the busy signal. He
hung up and leaned helplessly against the wall.

"She was a fresh little piece," the proprietor said. "Nowa-
days the eggs are smarter than the hens. You speak to her
politely, and she opens a mouth that—oh, well." He waved his
hand. "I was brought up differently. Once ..."

Franciszek again dialed his number. When he heard the
familiar voice of the switchboard operator, he breathed with
relief.

"This is Kowalski. Connect me with the party office,
please."

Once again he heard the busy signal—this time it was a
series of short rings.

"It's busy."

"I'll wait."

He pulled a chair over to him with his foot, and sat down.
The proprietor put down his newspaper. "Yes, sir, I had to
kiss my father's hands," he said. "The old man would say to

me, 'Janek'—my name is Jan—'you must obey your father, so your children will obey you later . . .' "

"Here's your party," the operator snapped. An instant later he heard a familiar voice: "Secretariat."

"This is Kowalski," Franciszek cried joyfully. "Is it you, Pawlak?"

"Yes. What's on your mind?"

"Listen, I've had a little trouble. I was detained."

"At the briefing?"

"No. In a police station."

"In connection with our city-to-village campaign?"

"No, just detained."

"Oh, I see—the deratization campaign."

"No, no—a supposed case of intoxication."

"But our delegate for the anti-drunkenness campaign is Cebulak. You are the city-to-village delegate."

"Listen to me; it had nothing to do with any campaign . . ." He leered at the proprietor, who kept staring at him with red-ringed eyes. "I—I—" he stammered. "It was personal . . ."

The voice in the receiver rose a tone higher. "You can act on your own, Comrade Kowalski, after the campaign. You're the city-to-village campaign delegate, and that's that. This must not happen again."

"All right," said Franciszek. "I'll come right over and explain. Goodbye."

"Goodbye."

Franciszek was hot; he felt himself suddenly drenched with sweat from his shirt down to his socks. He counted out the coins for the call. "A bottle of orangeade," he said.

The proprietor smiled with good-natured irony, as though to say, "Brother, who do you think you're kidding?"

"I haven't got any," he said. "There may be some kvass—"

"All right, make it kvass."

"I was saying there may be some kvass this afternoon. I have a bit of milk for my own personal use; I can let you have some."

"That's even better."

The proprietor tittered.

"What are you laughing about?"

"Here's your milk. I always try to understand everybody." And while Franciszek drank, the proprietor went on: "Don't take what happened to you too hard. They locked you up, and they let you go. I was locked up in 1945. I was in with a Russian major, a deserter, who had escaped dressed like a chimney sweep. 'Don't you ever get upset by anything, Vania,' he said to me—for my name is Jan—'don't be upset. Whatever they ask you, say you don't know. As for me, Vania'— my name is Jan—'this is the twenty-third time I've been locked up . . .' "

Franciszek put down his glass. "What do I owe you?"

"Wait a minute, I'll finish my story. 'You see, Vania,' he said, 'that's how many times I've been in jail.' "

"I'm in a hurry," Franciszek said. He glanced at the proprietor's unshaven face, and realized only then that this was how he too must look. "What do I owe you?" he shouted.

"Three-forty."

He paid and walked out.

"Hey, mister."

He turned around. The proprietor was waving to him with a mysterious expression. His stare was so compelling that Franciszek walked up to him, spellbound.

"I'll have coffee this afternoon . . ."

Once again he ran in his unbuttoned overcoat through the wet, muddy streets. He stopped suddenly. "And me?" he thought. "My name is Franciszek—" He heard the furious screech of brakes behind him, and jumped aside.

"What are you waiting for?" the driver screamed, "For applause?"

"For socialism," someone said on the sidewalk. The crowd roared with delight; Franciszek turned a bright red, and was about to answer something when he heard a familiar voice: "So you don't like it here? Come on, speak up: what is it you don't like?" He turned around: it was the same young sergeant who had picked him up the night before, and he was already reaching out for identification papers. Franciszek hunched his head between his shoulders and ran on in the direction of the tram stop, where a crowd of people were already lined up ahead of him in the rain.

# VI

HE TURNED IN AT HIS FACTORY, AND ENTERED THE porter's lodge. He thrust his card into the time clock, and it registered his tardiness. The mustachioed old porter walked up to him and, showing his yellowed teeth in a friendly smile, said, "The tramcar?"

"What tramcar?"

"You couldn't get on the tramcar?"

"Why do you ask?"

"You're late, Comrade Kowalski." He sighed, and spread his hands. "I'll have to keep your card," he added sadly.

Franciszek handed him his card. "Too bad."

He wanted to go, but the porter stopped him. "The best excuse you can give," he said in a dramatic whisper, "is the tramcar." He winked a brown eye; in the maze of white wrinkles it looked like a little star. "That can never be checked," he whispered; "the cars are always in such a mess . . ."

Franciszek muttered something unintelligible and went out. He walked along a blackened wall of bricks covered with posters showing the faces of smiling Stakhanovites; of peasants, men and women, with sheaves of grain; of schoolboys and soldiers; of diversionists and traitorous priests; of kulaks and saboteurs. They stared straight at his tired, unshaven face as though to ask, "Well, what now, my friend?" He had to close his eyes. Opening them, he saw before him a picture of an American soldier piercing a Korean child with his bayonet. The soldier looked like an orang-outang, and the child like a smaller species of monkey. He recoiled with a shudder, and almost groping his way reached the locker room. There he quickly put on a greasy gray apron, then went to the office of the party organization—it was situated in a barracks specially built by volunteer workers. He stopped before a door bearing a sign; once again he passed his hand over his unshaven face, smoothed his thinning hair, and, as though in an effort to master his weakness, knocked briskly.

"Come in," a voice boomed.

Franciszek walked in. A corpulent man with a friendly face rose from his seat behind the desk. He had the clay-colored complexion of those who never get enough to eat, live in stuffy rooms, and breathe large amounts of stale smoke. His cheeks were pendulous and his eyes red from constant lack of sleep; most of the people entrusted with looking after the souls of others have such faces. He held out his hand—it was heavy and hairy, but it squeezed Franciszek's warmly and cordially. "Take a seat," he said. After Franciszek sat down, he asked, "Well, what's the good word?"

"Good word?" Franciszek echoed. For a second he took the question to be ironical; then he looked at the secretary's tired, kindly face, and suddenly the nightmare he had been through seemed to him unreal—more than that, ridiculous. "But the whole thing is absurd," he thought. He sighed with relief: "Now at last I can have a sensible talk." He smiled for the first time in many hours. "I've had a little trouble," he said. "It was like this—"

There was a knock at the door. The secretary motioned to Franciszek to stop. "Just a minute . . . Come in."

A young boy, with a childlike face and charming bristling hair, walked in. Seeing Franciszek, he stood shifting his weight from foot to foot, as though about to withdraw.

"Come here, Blizniaczek," the First Secretary said cordially, and his heavy hand performed a circular motion. "Come closer; what the hell, sit down . . ." He pushed a chair over to the boy and gave him a friendly look. "What's the matter? Do they teach you to behave like a little girl in the Young Communist League, or what? Sit down; speak up, openly, like one of us, a workingman . . ."

The Young Communist Blizniaczek sat down. He glanced quickly at Franciszek, then stared at the tips of his shoes with great concentration. There was a long silence. Behind the walls the grinding machines hummed monotonously, like telegraph wires, a single protracted note.

"What is it, damn it?" the secretary asked at last. He smacked the table with the flat of his hand. "Are you going to open your mouth, or aren't you?"

"I'd like to talk to you privately," Blizniaczek stammered out.

The secretary shook his head. "This is an old comrade," he said solemnly. "You can say anything in his presence."

Blizniaczek looked at Franciszek with his blue eyes, shook his unruly hair, and said distinctly: "I want to report that Baniewicz and Majewska . . . well . . . you know what."

The secretary froze. A quick shudder passed over his face. He bent forward. "It's not true," he said hoarsely.

"It is."

The secretary banged his fist on the table so that everything shook. "Impossible."

Blizniaczek looked up at him with his clear blue eyes. "I am sure of it."

"How do you know?"

"I saw them."

"But ... Majewska has a husband and child."

Blizniaczek smiled triumphantly: "That's just it," he said. "That's just it."

"You saw them?"

"Yes. They have no apartment, that's why ... Yesterday, after work, in the warehouse—I saw it with my own eyes."

"Did they say anything?"

"Yes. I mean, Majewska told Baniewicz that she didn't love her husband but couldn't divorce him because he had a bad case of TB, and that someone has to look after him. And Baniewicz said that he had no apartment. And he said he didn't like the whole situation."

"So he doesn't like it?" To Franciszek the secretary's voice sounded like an echo.

"No."

The secretary rubbed his balding head and licked his lips. He had slumped forward; he looked like a man robbed of his most sacred belief. "A thing like that," he said, and his ringing bass sounded like an old man's whisper. "In the warehouse, after work ... And what did you do after work, Blizniaczek?"

"I conducted an informal talk," he said. "The subject was 'Love in the Life of the Soviet Man.' I was substituting for Plaskota; he substituted for me the other day, and he talked on 'The Forest in the Life of the Young Communist.'"

"In the warehouse, after work," the secretary repeated, not believing his own ears. "Baniewicz, our comrade ..." Once again he banged his fist on the table. Franciszek and Blizniaczek jumped up. "Here, on factory grounds!" he roared. He jumped up from behind his desk, and rushed around to Blizniaczek, holding out his hand. "Thank you in the name of the organization," he said, shaking his hand vigorously. "Poland will never forget what you've done for her. Goodbye."

Blizniaczek rose and walked in measured steps to the door. There he stopped for a moment, raising his left fist. "Where have I seen this before?" Franciszek thought suddenly. "Where have I seen it?"

Blizniaczek closed the door behind him, and walked down the corridor, his heels tapping. The secretary sat motionless for a while, his eyes vacant, unseeing. Then he turned to Franciszek; he remained silent. At last his eyes brightened again. "You see," he said in a tired voice, "here I sit behind my desk; everything seems to be all right; but wherever you look—the enemy is vigilant ..." He drummed on the glass plate with his clumsy fingers. "We must be vigilant," he said. "We must be constantly on our guard, Franciszek. Our people are inexperienced: they deviate; they succumb to whispering campaigns; it's easy to break them down ... Take Baniewicz. We sent him to the miners as an agitator—he did a good job. We sent him as our delegate to the scrap-collection campaign—he did well there too. He was top man in the clean-up Warsaw campaign; he even got a certificate. In our amateur theatricals he works like a fiend: he dances, sings, acts—some even say he has a good deal of talent. To look at him you'd say he was pure gold. And now, all of a sudden—plop!"

Once again he buried his face in his hands. His mouth drooped pitiably. "I shouldn't bother him at such a moment," Franciszek thought. But he swallowed hard, and said: "Listen, I'm late for work—I was out all morning. What I want to tell you won't take five minutes. Yesterday, as I was going home from the meeting, I met an old friend of mine from the underground, a wonderful fellow. He was deputy commander of our unit; now he's executive manager of a big construction project in the provinces somewhere." He paused, and sighed heavily. "That's all it was—an unexpected meeting, two old friends ... We went to a bar to talk about old times, and—there's no point hiding it—I drank a bit. Then we separated—"

Someone knocked at the door, and Franciszek stopped.

"Come in," said the secretary.

The door opened slightly; a man looked in, and, seeing that the secretary was not alone, was about to withdraw, but the secretary repeated, "Come in, come in."

A short man with a splendid shock of gray hair and nervous hands entered the room.

"I'm listening, Citizen Jarzebowski," the secretary said. "Make yourself at home, sit down."

The newcomer sat down, folding his nervous hands on his knees. His hair shone in the artificial light of the bulb.

"Well, what's on your mind, Citizen Jarzebowski?" the secretary asked. He glanced at Franciszek and tapped his forehead with his hand. "But of course you don't know each other, that's true. Our new head bookkeeper, Citizen Jarzebowski; Comrade Kowalski, assistant technical director. Citizen Jarzebowski is new here," he explained to Franciszek. "He's a nonparty activist. He is going to conduct a glee club as part of our social program."

"Yes, yes," Jarzebowski said eagerly, smiling at Franciszek. "Perhaps you'd like to join us?"

"What?"

"Would you do us the favor of joining our club and singing with us?"

"Me?" asked Franciszek, surprised.

"Why of course, what's so strange about that?" Jarzebowski said in a slightly offended tone. "What part would you like to sing? Baritone? Tenor? I suppose a baritone; you don't look like a bass—no offense meant. We're having our first rehearsal today after work—we're going to sing 'The March of the Enthusiasts.' How does it strike you?"

"I might at that if I can fit it in," Franciszek stammered.

Jarzebowski inclined his gray head with dignity. "I shall await your kind answer," he said.

The secretary said: "Well, what's on your mind, Citizen Jarzebowski? Speak up, come to the point; talk like one of us, a workingman."

"My dear sir," Jarzebowski stammered, turning red with pleasure, "this is a great honor—I mean, your kind expression, 'like one of us'—but you see, my dear sir," here he lowered his eyes with embarrassment, "unfortunately I am not with you because of my convictions; but, if I may say so, you will be good enough to understand, I hope—I am—I was—a landowner. I mean I have been a progressive since I was a boy, rather Left Wing, but . . ." He spread his arms in a magnificent gesture.

"Come now," the secretary said, "what are you trying to say?"

Jarzebowski cracked his knuckles—his nervous hands seemed to have a life of their own. "The fact is," he said dejectedly, "the fact is, I have nothing good to report. Please try to understand, this is not an easy thing for me to say; it's terribly unpleasant—please, understand me, dear sir, my situation is very, very delicate—but the duty of a Pole, a Left Winger . . ."

"Speak up; don't be afraid."

"A parcel," Jarzebowski blurted out.

"What parcel?"

"Malinowska, in the Bookkeeping Department. I mean,

my department," Jarzebowski added modestly, once again accompanying his words with a magnificent toss of his mane.

"Well, go on, what's next?"

"You've been good enough, if I may say so, to hit the nail on the head. That's just it: what next?"

"I don't understand."

Jarzebowski pounded his chest. "It's my fault, dear sir, my fault. Apparently I haven't been able to express myself clearly enough. Malinowska, of the Bookkeeping Department, received a parcel."

"Where from?"

Jarzebowski stood on his toes, raising his hands, as though addressing legions of witnesses. "That's the whole point," he said in a metallic voice. "A parcel from the West."

"From—the—We-e-est?"

"From the West. What's more, she makes no secret of it. She told me herself. She even treated me to a cigarette, which I have taken the liberty of bringing here ..." He reached into the upper pocket of his waistcoat, drew out a cigarette, and set it down in front of the secretary. "Please—here it is."

They stared at each other for a moment with piercing eyes. The secretary let out a whistle. "So that's how it is."

"Yes, indeed."

They remained silent. The clock on the wall ticked maddeningly. Somewhere in the factory a powerful engine was being tested at full speed; it stopped, only to start up again with an ear-splitting roar.

"A parcel," the secretary said pensively. Carefully, with the tips of his fingers, he picked up the cigarette and examined it from all sides; he turned it this way and that, sniffed it, and at last put it down, shaking his head. "A cigarette," he said; "the devil knows what that can lead to. That's how it always begins: parcels, cigarettes, nylons, a few trinkets, and then it turns out ..."

He paused, and his face tensed as if he were about to give birth to some powerful new idea, unique in form and expression. Jarzebowski held his breath; and to Franciszek, who was watching from the side, the secretary seemed to have become petrified. The suspense was palpable; even the clock seemed to be ticking more slowly.

"Thank you, Jarzebowski," the secretary said hoarsely after a while. "Our organization will take the matter up." He rose from his seat. "Thanks," he repeated. He shook the bookkeeper's hand vigorously, and as the latter turned his noble mane in the direction of the door, the secretary repeated once again, "Thank you, Citizen."

"Not at all," Jarzebowski said, and, turning to Franciszek, "How about our club?"

Franciszek clenched his jaw. "We'll see about that later," he said.

"Thanks," the secretary cried. He moved his chair over to Franciszek, patting him on the knee. "What do you think about it?"

He shrugged. "I don't know. Lots of people get parcels from abroad."

The secretary smiled jeeringly. "Parcels," he repeated. He leaned toward Franciszek, and lowered his voice to a whisper. "You don't know them."

"Whom do you mean?"

"*Them.*"

"But, damn it, the contents of the parcels are checked, aren't they?"

"You don't know them, and that's all there is to it," he said, keeping his superior smile. "Well, what's new with you? You were saying that you couldn't manage the campaign, weren't you?"

"It has nothing to do with the campaign," Franciszek said in a rage. "Yesterday I was detained in a police station, do you understand?"

"You? In a police station?"

"Yes."

"But why?"

Franciszek jumped to his feet. "Listen, Jan," he said, putting his hand on the other's arm. "You know me. Surely I don't have to tell you who I am and what I think, and why I am in the party. But yesterday I got horribly drunk ..." He walked a few steps, then turned his face toward the other. "Yesterday I insulted the party," he said in a wooden voice.

"You?"

"Me."

"But— But—" the secretary stammered. "What did you say?"

"I told them that they could stick it all up ..." Franciszek said, staring at the wall. "And I said something much worse, but even they, in the station, were ashamed to repeat it. And I myself don't remember. I was in a blur for a minute, so furious I was out of my head, and everything I said left my mind; nothing remains—a blank."

"Man, man," the secretary was stammering. "What have you done? What police station was that?"

"Forty-two."

"Ah," the secretary said with sudden relief. "Well, my friend, you're lucky. I'll ring them up at once; I have a friend there, a colleague—we may be able to fix it."

He picked up the receiver; Franciszek restrained his hand. "No," he said, "that's not what I want, Jan."

"Well?"

"I don't want to settle the matter that way, Jan. They took everything down in black and white—that I'm an enemy." He shook his head. "This must be handled differently. At the moment I can't trust myself. The party must look into this."

"The party?"

"Yes. It's up to our comrades to say that I'm right. They've got to tell me that they trust me, the way they have always trusted me up till now. And that my position here is justified. There's a meeting tomorrow. I want you to put the case on the agenda. Listen—I've got a son, a grown son, who's in the party. I have a daughter who will also join the party someday. My children must believe in me. I don't want anyone to tell them, 'Your father's the kind of fellow who says one thing, and thinks another ...' I don't think that way. I never thought that way—or else I wouldn't be here, with you, now. Unity of thought and word and deed, that's what makes a man. To my mind that's the meaning of loyalty ... Do you understand me, Jan?"

"I understand, of course; I understand," the other said. He was staring at the window; a wretched gray light seeped through the pane, trying to assert itself against the crazily flickering bulb on the ceiling. The secretary pressed his head with his hands. "What a filthy day it is!" he said. "First you, then Baniewicz with Majewska, then this parcel ... You look at it superficially—the parcel is fine. It's labeled, sealed, passed —that's the end of it, you might think. But hell knows what it may lead to ..." He looked heavily at Franciszek. "Damn it all!" he said in a fury. "Haven't I enough troubles? Just tell me. First it's Baniewicz, then it's a parcel, now it's some other dirty business—to hell with it all ..." He drummed on the table with his fingers; the terrible roar of the engines in the workshops went on and off. "Why did you have to blurt it out?" the secretary asked.

Franciszek froze suddenly, as though coated with ice. "What did you say?" he growled.

"Why did you have to talk?" the secretary went on, staring at the dusty windowpanes. "Listen to me: Are you a party comrade? You are. Have you a card? You have. Have you a job? You have. Well, damn it, behave like a party comrade. But instead you suddenly scream at the top of your lungs, 'I believe, I don't believe, stick it all up ...' Goddam it, who asked you to go into all that?"

He drew aside just in time: a heavy brass weight flew by a few inches from his face. The windowpane tinkled; the roar of the engines surged into the room with new intensity.

"Bastard!" Franciszek hissed, coming close to the other, his fingers outspread like claws. "You! Our First Secretary! Talking like that! I'll show you ... tomorrow ... at the meeting. I'll tell everybody ..." He walked toward the door through a roaring red haze.

"Franciszek!" the other cried. "Franciszek, but I haven't—"

As the door opened, he ran into Blizniaczek.

# VII

THE MEETING OF THE PARTY ORGANIZATION OF the "For a Better Tomorrow" automobile repair shop opened at five the next afternoon. Franciszek barely had time to eat his dinner in the canteen and to wash up. Buttoning his coat on the way, he ran to the crowded meeting room. The hall was too small for the crowd, and there was so much smoke that the open, smiling faces of the dignitaries in the portraits on the wall were scarcely visible behind the thick haze; and in the joyful faces of the Stakhanovites, boys and girls, there was something mysterious, unfathomable, as in the faces in portraits by old masters. At the table, covered with red cloth of the kind used for flags—it was riddled with cigarette holes—sat the First Secretary, Comrade Pawlak; his deputy, a young engineer with a face that twitched like a rabbit's; two members of the Executive Committee; and a delegate from the party's district organization. Franciszek pushed his way through the chairs, found an empty one, and sat down. His case was the third item on the agenda. The First Secretary silenced the room by an imperious motion of his hand, and rose. "I declare the meeting open." He held out his hands to applaud, but before he had brought them together the whole room was clapping. This went on a long while. Then the applause subsided.

"Since there are no objections, the meeting is open," he said, and his ringing voice filled every corner of the smoky room. "On the agenda we have the self-criticism of Comrade Jablonka, the cases of comrades Gierwatowski and Kowalski, ad lib motions, and discussion. Does any comrade wish to supplement the agenda?"

Before anyone had time to reply, he clapped his hands. The general applause lasted several minutes. Then Comrade Jablonka took the floor.

"Comrades," he began in a high, tense voice. "I'll simply say, in our working-class way, that I went off the deep end. No matter what anyone thinks and thinks, the best thing for a decent man is to admit right away, I went off the deep end, and that's all there is to it. Sometimes a man thinks to himself, Maybe I ought to do this or that; but I'm not like that; I speak straight in our workingman's way—I went off the deep end, and that's all there is to it. Thoughts of all kinds come to me. I don't know why. And yet a man sometimes thinks this or that, and it turns out that he has gone off the deep end. So I'll simply say like a workingman—I went off the deep end, and that's that." He raised his voice. "Comrades," he cried. "There was starvation, there was capitalism, there was misery: people were hungry, bloated, I saw it myself, with my own eyes, comrades. Then along came a man named Lenin. And the people woke up, comrades. And we ourselves know how things are, and we also know that they'll be better. And I went off the deep end, comrades. When I was little, I tore wings from beetles and from flies; and I did things with cats and frogs that—well, to put it bluntly—I had fun that wasn't our kind, the workers' kind. Once a man died under my window. And it's well known, comrades, that Comrade Stalin said: 'Man—the word has a proud ring.' There were terrible times. There was starvation, and misery, and capitalism; until a man named Lenin came along. And once again, comrades—my shop will deliver the shovels on time."

He stopped. The audience awoke. The room shook with cheers. Everybody was clapping. Even those who had been overcome by sleep at the beginning of the meeting looked about them with wide-open bewildered and terrified eyes, and clapped harder than the others, trying to wake up as quickly as possible, to drive the last shreds of sleep from their eyelids, and to participate in the life of the meeting. Some comrades had tears in their eyes, and were sniffling loudly, reaching for their handkerchiefs. The aged leader of the solderers' group awoke too late; rubbing his eyes violently, he cried, "Long live—" Someone added at once, "Long live the Soviet solderers—the builders of the Dneprostroi!" The cry was at once taken up by the entire audience, and for several minutes shouts went up from a hundred throats in honor of the builders of the Dneprostroi, Magnitogorsk, and Komsomolsk; of the Donbas miners; of the Kuban Cossacks; the Ukraine kolkhozniks; the Byelorussian guerrillas; the Soviet scientists; the Sevastopol sailors; the heroic defenders of Stalingrad; the explorers of the Arctic Circle; Lysenko, Michurin, and Olga Lepeshchinskaya; the clamor concluded with hurrahs in honor of Joseph Stalin's works in the field of linguistics.

After Jablonka's self-criticism, the atmosphere in the room grew warm and cordial. People smiled at each other, exchanged cigarettes, and made animated and approving comments on Jablonka's speech. After a moment of confusion, almost unavoidable in such cases, the First Secretary took the floor. He stated in a few words his opinion of Jablonka's case, and spoke appreciatively of the man's sincerity and courage. The next item on the agenda was the case of Comrade Gierwatowski.

But before Gierwatowski, who had risen from his seat, had time to collect his thoughts and speak, someone cried out: "Comrade Nowak has an Airedale terrier called Sambo. I ask you, why Sambo? We must put a stop to this, once and for all."

Franciszek recognized the voice of the young Blizniaczek.

"That should be in the ad lib motions," people cried. "The ad lib motions!"

"Why wait?" others cried. "Such things must be settled at once. One day it's Sambo, and the next day—what? Throwing napalm bombs on Korean children, maybe?"

"More vigilance, comrades!"

"Disgusting!"

"Sambo! Why not Bombo?"

"So that's where you get your inspiration, Nowak?"

"Put a stop to all this!"

"There was starvation, there was misery, there was capitalism . . ."

"Hand in your party card!"

"It was people like you that shot women and children in Korea!"

Comrade Nowak stood up and explained in a trembling voice that he had bought the dog after it had been named, and that when he tried to call it Bouquet the dog did not react, and on one occasion even bit Nowak's mother-in-law on the leg; but he promised that beginning today he would call his dog Red, no matter what happened. After a moment of extraordinary tumult, the meeting was resumed.

"Comrades," began Gierwatowski, a gray-haired locksmith with a mighty mustache, "I'll speak briefly, in our working-class way. I am a simple man, and I don't like fancy talk. So I'll ask plainly: Is it true that peoples come from monkeys?"

The audience was dumbfounded. People stared at one another in consternation. The eyebrows of the district delegate rose to his hairline; the Second Secretary's face looked more like a rabbit's than ever. The first to speak was Blizniaczek— he was at the meeting as the delegate of the Young Communist League. "Comrade Zamodzinski collects the labels of bottles," he said.

"Not now, Comrade Blizniaczek," several voices interrupted him. "This should come in the ad lib motions. Let Gierwatowski speak. Speak up, Comrade Gierwatowski."

"Speak up," the district delegate said.

"Speak up," Pawlak said.

"Speak up," Blizniaczek said simultaneously with the Second Secretary.

"Well, I am speaking," said Gierwatowski. "Is it true that peoples come from monkeys?"

"*People*, not *peoples*, Comrade Gierwatowski," Blizniaczek corrected him.

"What?"

"People."

"That's what I am saying: peoples."

"Just a moment," the district delegate said; his eyebrows had returned to their initial position. "In just what connection are you asking this?"

"Well, how can it be? Peoples from monkeys?"

"What of it?"

Gierwatowski grew red with anger. "My son comes to me and says, 'Daddy, is it true that peoples come from monkeys?' 'Clear out, you little squirt,' I say to him, 'or I'll give you a kick in the ass that'll make you forget your monkeys. Back to your homework.' 'But that's what they're teaching,' he says. 'It's in the book; it really is.' 'Where?' I say. 'It's a long time since you've been spanked.' 'Here,' he says. I pick up the book, I read, and I can't believe my eyes. I read, and I think, Have I gone nuts in my old age? Or has the fellow that printed this gone crazy? That's what it says in the book—from monkeys, and that's all there is to it. I hit the brat over the head, and on Sunday I went to the zoo myself." He paused.

"Well?"

"Is it possible?"

"Is what possible?"

"That we come from monkeys?"

Blizniaczek rose to his feet; his hair bristled like a brush. "What do you want, Gierwatowski? Isn't it all the same to you who your great-great-grandfather was? It's not a question of social origins, but of science. That's how you've got to look at it."

Gierwatowski's face darkened; his neck was purple, and his mustache jerked up. "Damn you!" he roared. "Shut up, you hoodlum! My grandfather was a blacksmith at Gerlach's, and don't you wipe your dirty mouth with him." He shook an enormous fist.

There were shouts: "Boring from within!" "We must be vigilant!" "A foreign agent!" "No use going easy with him! Report him to the security police!" "An enemy!" "How many dollars did you get for that, Gierwatowski?" "We know your kind: here you talk about monkeys, and the moment our backs are turned you throw sand in the machines!" "Comrades, don't let him pull the wool over our eyes!" "There was starvation, there was misery, there was ..."

"Quiet, comrades!" the district delegate cried. He turned

to Gierwatowski: "Your case will be taken up by the Executive ..." He stared at him for a while. "The party didn't expect this of you," he said dryly. "You'll suffer the consequences."

Gierwatowski sat down, dazed. The First Secretary announced: "The case of Comrade Kowalski."

# VIII

FROM THE DARK STREETS THE WIND BLEW SUDDENLY, picking up tatters of old posters and dragging them across the square. The second shift had begun; he could hear the roar of the engines, and the rattling and grinding of the machines. He passed the gate and walked out into the street; it ran far off into the darkness, and somewhere at the end of it drunks were staggering under the gas lamps, their shadows shrinking and crawling along the ground, or lengthening and sliding over the unlit windows of the houses. The sidewalk was wet and glassy. Franciszek looked down; in the puddles stars swam like fat worms. A pimp emerged from a passageway. "Your honor," he said, tipping his cap, "I have a nice girl for you tonight."

Franciszek pushed him away silently, and walked on. He raised his head and breathed in the air with all his strength; there was a lump of steel in his lungs. He walked on, occasionally stumbling; he stared at the sky—it was better, easier this way. An insipid moon was drifting over the roofs; the darkness grew thicker and thicker, a clammy, impenetrable darkness which choked the sickly stars and the crowded city. A military patrol tramped by, their heels clattering. The moon suddenly dropped out of sight behind a dirty cloud; the soldiers walked ahead, staring apprehensively into the damp darkness.

... The end. Period. We had the same moon then. It was spring—a premature, sickly spring like this one. The sky was gray, the earth was black, the trees were black too; only the bullet marks, as bright and fresh as milk, spoke of spring. Yes, that was the way it was. I was standing with Jerzy in front of our dugout. We had a good dugout, with a pine ceiling, and a requisitioned couch; there must have been forty of us sleeping in that dugout. Jerzy told me to go to the estate, two or three miles away, pretend this was an official requisition, and bring back some lard and flour. I picked three boys, and we were about to leave—the darker, the better; the later, the better; for the faces of people met at night are quickly forgotten, though the first impression is more vivid. We were leaving when the medic came out. "Bring some liquor that we can use for disinfecting the wounds," he said, and handed us a canister. I was angry. "You want me to go to a bar?" I asked. "Don't be an ass: there's a still a few hundred yards this side of the estate. I know the owner; he is one of us, and lives in the little house next door. He won't ask questions. He's helped before." I took the canister; the dull face of the moon was reflected in the white tin. I shuddered—there was something repulsive about all this. "Are you cold?" Jerzy asked. "No," I said. "I'll give you my sheepskin," he said. "Thanks, I'll manage." And off we went. There were four of us—myself and the three boys. We carried knapsacks, the biggest we could get. The boys were young—two from the village, and one, a wiseguy from Cracow, whom I didn't like. He had a couple of gold teeth and a rat's face; his hands were sweaty, and he often rubbed them with alcohol, infuriating the medic by wasting the precious supply. Our commander, too, hit him over the head a few times. But why do I remember him so well? ...

Next to a wall a drunk lay on the ground, his face in his own vomit. Franciszek stopped without thinking and bent over him; he shook the arm of the unconscious man, but he lay like a log. On the wall someone had chalked in block letters: "Manka is a whore. Ground floor, ring twice." A little farther on, there was an inscription, "Hands off Korea." And still farther, "These premises free of mines. Sergeant Blotniak." The dim lights of an automobile moved silently along the slippery pavement. Over the city blazed a fiery neon sign: YOUNG PEOPLE READ *THE BANNER OF YO  H*. Two letters had burned out long ago—it was like a mouth with teeth missing. Franciszek walked on. A girl with the face of a corpse said to him: "Hey, honey, where you going, baby?"

Farther on there were mud and concentrated darkness. Franciszek trudged on, sloshing stupidly through the mud. In a ground-floor window lights were burning; the brittle shadows of dancers drifted across the curtain; a loudspeaker was screeching *On the bridge across the river* . . . Someone was knocking at the house door: "Mr. Skowron, Mr. Skowron . . ." Franciszek turned to the left. Here was light—sharp, brilliant, hissing: some workers were soldering the tram rails at a crossing; drenched in blue light, wearing blue masks, they looked like ghosts.

. . . Now I know why I didn't like that boy: he was a practical joker; he knew thousands of tricks—he had one for every day, for every occasion—and millions of jokes. Once he told me—once? it was that very night. Twenty-five workers armed with enormous tongs are carrying a long steel rail. "Hey-oop, hey-oop," they shout. The rail is moving forward, inch by inch. The foreman comes in and shakes his head. "That's not the way to do it, boys." He picks up the rail, and carries it unaided for twenty yards. The workers smile contemptuously.

"That's nothing but brute strength," they say; "what counts is the know-how." The squirt. That night he talked more than ever, and finally I told him to shut up. The village was not far away; we turned into a path leading to the still. After we had knocked for a long time, the owner came out. He had thrown a sheepskin over his night clothes, his face was puffy with sleep, and he kept blinking his eyes—I thought I would go mad looking at those flapping eyelids. He took us to the vat, where each one of us had a good drink; we filled our canister, and set out again. The owner, scratching his hairy chest, asked: "How long are we going to wait for freedom?" I said something that didn't make much sense—the more a man fights, the less he worries about freedom. And again we pushed on through the mud, clinging to the fences; at last we were at the manor. The house was neither rich nor poor; but, judging from the neat paths, the white fences, the carefully trimmed flower beds, and the straw-wrapped trees, the place gave the impression of being run by a martinet. "Check your guns," I said, and the next moment I could hear the clicking of locks. I had no tommy gun myself, only an ordinary revolver, a heavy old thing that made a good deal of noise. They all laughed at me; they liked the Parabellum and the fifteen-shot FN; I always preferred my old block-buster that never failed me; an automatic is always in danger from water, sand, the slightest bit of rust; a revolver will fire even in mud. We knocked at the door for a long time—the boys were beginning to get anxious—when at last a woman came out. She screamed and fussed a bit, and then another woman, the one who owned the place, appeared, her arms spread wide. "I haven't a thing, gentlemen," she said; "I just barely keep body and soul together." And suddenly—plop, she fainted. There was a vase of flowers—God knows how she got flowers at that season—I splashed water in her face. When she showed signs of coming to, I said to the boys: "Go to the storeroom; I'll look after her." They went in. I knelt beside her, and saw her wide-open deceitful eyes—she had Germans waiting for us. In no time they killed the three who had gone to the storeroom—a bit of shooting, smoke, noise. I plugged a bullet into a German's stomach—he was no more than a few inches away. I rushed to the porch—a spray of bullets had riddled the wall right above me—and the first thing I did was to grab the canister of alcohol. I ran several hundred yards with it, and dropped it only when a furious light burst in my lungs, lighting up everything inside and outside for a fraction of a second. I ran on, clutching my revolver, as if I were running into the very center of the sun—into the rain, the mud, and the night torn to shreds by the firing. A dog was roused, and ran after me howling; then a second, and a third; then all the dogs in the universe were running after me through the mud; I felt my blood inside my belt, then in my trousers, then in my socks. I didn't know whether I would have enough strength to get away into the night, the woods, the trees, with my breath cut to pieces, and a lump of lead somewhere near my heart and lungs—I felt it more and more strongly; it grew inside me with every step, like a living body. I knew only one thing—I've got to run, get as close as I can to my own people; to run and to try not to stumble, because if my knees once gave way under me, that would be my last step ... Somewhere behind me, splashing against the glassy shield of the sky, blind and full of hatred in the wet night, a machine gun was rattling ...

Two policemen passed in the middle of the roadway. Their steel badges gleamed dully. Imprisoned in the circle of a flashlight, Franciszek crossed the street. Once again he walked along a moldy wall covered with posters that flapped in the stinking wind, threatening, admonishing, persuading; carrying the entire contents of the world, they hung there precariously in the empty blustery night. Somewhere at the end of the night a song rang out. Franciszek turned his head; the solid shadows of the two policemen had merged with a third, fluid shadow; the song evaporated, changed into a stammer; and the night sucked it in, along with the water flowing in the gutters.

"Watch out!" someone cried behind him. "Where are your eyes?"

He stopped. A large hole, left uncovered by sewer diggers, gaped at his feet. At the bottom of the ditch the damaged pipes gurgled happily and emitted a strong stench.

"Thanks," said Franciszek. "Good night."

"Good night."

He touched the brim of his hat; it was sodden and slippery.

... In the end I did fall, after I don't know how many agonizingly painful steps through the darkness. I crawled, in the mud and water, toward the woods, where the darkness was thickest. Now I felt no pain; I thought only of the mud; I was all clogged up with mud—I felt it in my mouth, my eyelids, my nose and ears; I was tormented by the absurd thought that the mud would get into my lungs—perhaps through my wound. Behind me came dogs, shots, and hurried splashing steps. I turned over on my side; I saw dark figures running toward me across the bare slippery fields. How many were there? How many yards separated them from me? I didn't know; I knew only one thing: there are moments when a man feels suddenly that he has been stripped of everything, that all he has left is only one thought; he wouldn't even be able to summon other thoughts—my one thought was how to save my last bullet for myself. I didn't trust my hands; a soldier's finger is too quick on the trigger. I pulled a bullet out of the chamber, and thrust it into my mouth. Then I rested my hand with the revolver on some damn' mound of earth; I aimed at the closest of my pursuers; I aimed a long time—a second, the fraction of a second—an eternity; then something tore at my hand, and the running man suddenly doubled up and dropped head first into the mud like a rabbit. It sounded like a big dog licking his chops. Once again I pressed the trigger—I was distinctly aware of the sweetish, coppery taste of the bullet I was holding in my mouth—and once again my hand jerked, and the muzzle of my gun jumped up, short and rigid like a boxer's head. I saw a gleam on the other side—a kind of yellow glow. Suddenly a fountain of mud exploded in my face, spraying my eyes; I raised my hand to rub them, and then it was as if a great knife had severed everything, the whole shell of the world—the pain, the firing, the bullets, the noise, and the gloomy darkness over the nearby woods . . .

"Screw me!" a drunken woman cried. He was passing a smelly doorway. "You may be a carpenter, but you're no St. Joseph." There was a tussle; the man hit her in the face; the blow sounded as loathsome and sticky as the echo of the footsteps in the mud; Franciszek shuddered as though suddenly drenched in cold water.

. . . I was dying. A fellow who had been a carpenter in civilian life made a stretcher for me—a filthy wooden litter stinking with my blood and pus. As they carried me I begged them to destroy those boards after everything was over, after I'd given up the ghost, and not to touch them even for a minute. I was dying; I knew it, and so did the others—Jerzy, our commander, and all the boys who dragged me from place to place, stumbling over roots in the forest, over holes in the muddy roads, and sinking to the waist in the slush, pressed down by the weight of my carcass. They were saying that I was dying; they asked each other, "Is he still breathing?" There were marches, longer stops, stops for rest, narrow escapes. One day, at a place where we stayed for some time, a few boys were admitted to the party. It's difficult to explain why they should have wanted to be; they had excellent chances of reaching eternity next day by any number of roads; but this short ceremony was the only reality in the lives of any of us, a reality toward which we all marched, or which marched toward us; this, nothing else. I asked for Jerzy; he was and will always be the man closest to me. All sorts of people have a place in our hearts—we can take them or leave them; those we love leave a scar. He came, slender, calm, cool.

"How are you?" he asked.

"Fine. And what about her, Jerzy?"

"Her? Who do you mean?"

"The woman that owned the place."

"What do you think? Just a couple of days later."

"There, on her estate?"

"No, in town."

"Had you arranged the requisition with her?"

"Of course. Why do you bring that up?"

"I'm going to die."

"Don't be too sure."

"I'm sure. And first I want to know: who got her?"

"I did."

"You?"

"I can die any time, too. I've got to settle everything first, everything there is to be settled."

We were silent for a while. I remember where we had our talk—the smoky interior of a hut. In the corner, an old woman was muttering prayers; a forlorn cat was crawling on the window sill.

"Jerzy, are boys being admitted to the party today?"

"Two."

"Take me in with them."

He did not answer; he bent over me and looked at me fixedly. Without averting his eyes, he said in the same neutral tone, "We don't know whether you'll get out of this." He smiled. He took the cat on his knees and stroked its flat head. "What use are dead people to the party?"

"If that's the kind of man you are," I said, "I'm glad I'm saying goodbye to you."

He rose.

"You can tell each other jokes at my funeral," I said.

"We don't hold funerals," he said. "There's never enough time."

He put the cat down gently, and walked away. I hovered between life and death, at some undefined point of existence, helpless, without a will, like a bird driven by a high wind; I vomited, I raved, I averted my eyes from the dressings stiff with my blood; the hours, the days, the weeks were like a rubber band stretched to the breaking point. I begged for life, for death, for medicines, for a gun; I choked with hatred for others who paid me back in kind, burdened as they were with my emaciated body that aroused their contempt—a bundle of pale purple bones covered with yellow skin. Then came a day when I knew I was ready to die every day at dawn if need be: I knew I was alive. I was already moving about unaided.

"Well," Jerzy asked one day, "are you all right now?"

"Yes."

He sat down. He began to roll a cigarette, frowning desperately. He had never learned to roll a cigarette properly, although his fingers were skillful and strong. In all the years of partisan warfare he had still not mastered an art that every boy learns in a week. I saw that his eyes were angry as he bent over his recalcitrant piece of paper. At last he lighted it. "Do you know why I talked like that—then?" he asked.

"It's none of my business. You're the commander. I don't want to slosh around in your conscience."

He smiled. "Listen," he said. "I didn't want you to think of the party as a sacrament. We're at war; we must think about how to win it and survive. You've got to live, Franciszek; for people like you the war won't be over soon, perhaps never. You can depend on a man's will to live only if he has something to look forward to, something he wants to possess or to be a part of. Revenge, a man, a woman—something must get into your blood and say to you: Stand up and fight. When your life was running so low, you hadn't made up your mind about that. Now you can go ahead; the sooner, the better."

"You're a hard man, Jerzy," I said. "And what if I had reported to the clouds?"

He shrugged. "We would have given you a funeral, anyway," he said. "Though you know yourself that there's no time for such things."

"You're a hard man," I repeated. "It takes a special kind of courage to talk like that."

He struggled with his cigarette, rerolling the treacherous paper over and over. "I don't know what courage really is," he said. Despite his efforts, his cigarette kept falling apart. "I've thought about it all my life. As a boy, I had a different idea of it—rescuing somebody from fire or water, performing a heroic action in war, raping my grandmother, that kind of thing. Now these things have to be reconsidered. All the usual opinions about courage are based on the idea of exceptional circumstances. But at bottom a man's behavior in battle or during a fire tells us nothing about him, but only shows how he reacts in such situations. In abnormal circumstances you get abnormal reactions; nothing that can be foreseen, and nothing to be surprised at."

"Is there such a thing as normal courage?"

He was silent for a moment; his cigarette had disintegrated for good. He rolled the remnants of tobacco between his fingers. "I think there is," he said. "Courage is probably just a matter of faith. People are nothing but a herd of swine wallowing in a sea of shit. It's easy to define man in his lower aspects—he is infinitely beastly; he is capable of everything; he'll believe everything and befoul everything. Courage in the truest sense is ability to find man's upper, ultimate limits—the extent to which he can be trusted and is capable of achievement. That is how I understand Communism. As for you, I was sure you'd pull through."

"In order to kill?"

"In the name of life."

"And our enemies?"

"What about our enemies?"

"Don't they think the same way?"

He shrugged again. "I don't know what they think," he said. "I only know in the name of what they kill, and that is what matters to me in this war. I know what they did to man, and I know what I want man to be: this entitles me to take part in the game. I want an epoch and an earth that will make it possible for man to be truly courageous. That's the only thing I'm interested in." He rose; his boots creaked unpleasantly. "While the war is on, don't try to find justifications that don't exist," he said. "The only thing you can do is to think about the world you want to go back to, the place you want to live in. Distance between dream and reality defines a man's morality, nothing more. Haven't you got a decent cigarette?"

He lighted one. We set out. Where? To what place of life, dream, war? I don't remember. We were approaching a little town; there were only a few of us. We were supposed to find somebody in the market, a fellow who thought he was terribly smart, a secret agent of the Gestapo, and to blast him out of existence. It was noon. The August air was thick as cheese. When we emerged from the woods and saw the town spread out below us—a dirty little place—bells began to ring, gloomy and helpless in the torrid air. Then a factory siren began to wail; as far as I know there was only one factory in this hole.

"The siren operator must have been asleep," Jerzy said.

"Why? Maybe he let the church have priority."

"You go to the left, and we'll go to the right . . ."

The taxicab stopped with a screech a few steps behind Franciszek. He jumped aside like a rabbit. The driver, furious, leaned out the window. "Didn't you hear my horn?"

"I'm sorry; I was thinking," Franciszek said, staring at his mud-spattered overcoat.

"Where are you going?" the driver asked. His motor gave off black fumes. "Want a lift?"

"Thanks," Franciszek said. "I'll walk."

The car rolled on, and vanished beyond the street corner. After a few dozen yards the street was suddenly all lit up. A night shift was working on a building; elevators whirred inside the stone walls; platforms swinging like big formless birds moved slowly upward; the green light of drilling crews gleamed from dark scaffoldings that merged with the empty sky—lumpy human spiders amid showers of burning metal. Compressors hissed monotonously in the ditches; a sign said:

"THIS MONTH WE HAVE FULFILLED . . ." The figures were hidden in the shadows.

"Where are you going?" cried someone he could not see. "No loitering here; this is a construction project."

. . . "We build everything from the foundations up—if I may use big words—from the very fundamentals." Someone—who was it?—had said that at the meeting. "We are building something in the name of which people have died not by dozens and not by hundreds, but by whole generations. The struggle for social justice began the moment two people first met in the world. Socialism is the final form of this struggle (applause); the sacrifices made by the party (applause), the martyrs of socialism (applause) . . ." A short interruption—and what next? . . .

He was tired; he was dragging himself through the night and its murky echoes; a dark wave was pulsing within him, growing stronger and stronger. Now he was walking across a vacant lot, through aseptically clean places, with a lump of lead in his head; he could not strike a single spark in himself. He wanted only one thing—to relive the moment he had experienced a few hours earlier, although between that moment and now there was a whole life—years, oceans, worlds of defeat, loneliness, exhaustion, futility. Thus reviewing the different areas of his life, he was unable to fix them in time: the past, the present, memories and facts, everything was fluid, incomprehensible; he thought only of that moment which was the kernel of the universe—the moment when someone had told him to turn in his party card. That was real—as real as the street he was walking in, as real as the shabby dawn beginning to creep over the stones of the city, as real as the visible and persuasive neon sign, YOUNG PEOPLE READ—wherever he might hide, sit down, or stop. He raised

his head—YOUNG PEOPLE READ *THE BANNER OF YO  H*—
and gasped for air. He wanted to think, he wanted to remember, but he could do nothing now; his thoughts were turning
in a void—it was like trying to strike a spark with two damp
stones. All he could recall was the moment when he rose and
looked at the audience, but he could remember nothing he
had said or done. He wanted to think, to set the machine of
his awareness in motion; he wanted something to put him on
the right track. He picked up a crumpled newspaper from the
sidewalk, and stopped under a street lamp. "Tarnow Already
Ahead." "The world camp . . ." "Polish Youth Flings a Powerful No in Kałużyński's Face." He walked, the newspaper dangling from his hand. This helped—the familiar words, always
arranged the same way, sounding always the same, had put
his thoughts on the right track; he had been there before, he
remembered. The rest, like the date of the newspaper, had
no importance.

    . . . "We imagine that the most painful thing that can hap-
pen to us is when someone dear to us dies. He leaves an empty
place behind; we love, we respect, we cherish; and sometimes
years go by before the place is somehow filled and the pain
is gone. But worse than death, comrades, is to be betrayed by
a man who is close to us; it is more painful, for we ourselves
are responsible for that empty and painful place in our lives"
(long, heavy applause)—who had said that? Pawlak? The Second Secretary? The district delegate? Someone in the audience? Whose voice was that? Now I am walking through the
city; I pass by unknown people, drunks, thieves, lovers—and
someone spoke to me, someone who had power, whom others trust, someone who could strike me from party member-
ship. Before that it was day; after that it was night; now there
will be dawn—who said that? Somewhere among the walls of

this city is my house to which I shall return—changed; somewhere—to the right, to the east or the west—is my place of
work, where I shall go presently—changed; all around me are
alien people—but who said that? (Long, heavy applause.) "An
accident has unmasked you. You said what you really think.
I checked it with the police station, and I won't dare repeat
what you had said (cries of indignation), what you screamed
(here someone applauded, by mistake; cries of fury and indignation); I have too much respect for what we all believe
in. You're an alien." An alien. Do we come from monkeys?
There was starvation, there was capitalism, there was misery.
I ask you, comrades, why Sambo? Such people use napalm
bombs in Korea. Had it not been for an accident, you'd still be
among us; you'd go on doing your dirty work—a former partisan, officer, party comrade. And then came a man named
Lenin. Those who are for the expulsion of Comrade Kowalski,
let them show their party cards. Step out, Comrade Kowalski.
Come in, Kowalski. Why Sambo? Now it's a dog, and what
will it be later on? People, not peoples, from monkeys. Hand
in your card, Kowalski; don't make a monkey of yourself; we
know you're clever at wearing masks. May this accident be a
lesson to you, comrades, that at every moment of our lives,
in every situation, we must be vigilant. This is what the party
demands of us. This is what the great Stalin teaches us. Well,
and how about our glee club? We begin tomorrow . . .

"He's drunk," a boy cried. "A big man like that! Blubbering
like a baby!"

The sidewalks were filled with people; the factory sirens
were howling, and the sounds vanished somewhere under
the cardboard sky. A crowded noisy tramcar clattered by. The
neon sign over the city went out.

# IX

HE WAS WIFELESS; HIS WIFE HAD DIED A FEW weeks after the end of hostilities; though of poor health, she had managed to stay alive until his return from the woods. He lived with his son and daughter. His son's name was Mikołaj, his daughter's Elzbieta. Mikołaj, a magnificently handsome boy, was twenty-four; Elzbieta was younger. They occupied two small rooms in a new housing project. The day after the meeting, when Franciszek came home, he found his daughter with her fiancé, Roman. They attended the same courses, and planned to marry immediately after getting their degrees. Both looked happy.

"Got something for supper?" Franciszek asked. He stood in the middle of the room without removing his overcoat and hat.

"I'll warm up something for you," Elzbieta said. She rose. She was tall, towheaded, attractive. Franciszek's heart sometimes tightened when he looked at her: he had the feeling that he was seeing the woman with whom he had lived his happiest moments twenty years earlier. No one could have discovered any difference between Elzbieta and her mother; both were the image of health, though both spent their time complaining. "I'll warm the macaroni for you," Elzbieta said. "I can make you an omelet too." She went to the kitchen. Franciszek sat down stiffly on a chair.

"Well, Pop," said Roman, a black-haired, swarthy boy with fiery eyes, "what's the matter? Troubles?" Roman called Franciszek "little father-in-law," "old man," or "Pop." The dry and forbidding Franciszek forgave him much for the sake of his daughter's love-drenched eyes.

"Everybody has troubles," he said, and broke off, crushed by the stupidity of his own words.

"Clever observation," Roman said. "Elzbieta and I got drunk today."

Franciszek started. "Really?"

"Really. We drank a bottle of wine after passing our exams. Ha-ha-ha."

Franciszek sighed with relief. "Thank God."

"What?"

"Thank God."

"A metaphysical notion. You surely know, Pop, that religion is opium for the masses. You know that, don't you?"

"Yes."

"And who said it?"

"I'm tired," Franciszek said gently. "Let me alone, Romek."

"You just don't remember. That's bad, bad. Once your memory begins to fail, you can make all sorts of blunders. Lenin wrote brilliantly about memory. It's in a letter to a friend, saying he needed money for an abortion."

Franciszek opened his eyes wide. "Roman, what are you talking about? Where did he write that?"

Roman expressed surprise. "Don't you remember?"

"No."

"Come, come."

"Really, I don't."

Roman wrung his hands. "Why, that's impossible."

"My word of honor."

Roman laughed triumphantly. "Of course it's not true," he said. "I just wanted to see whether you'd be taken in by such rot."

He went on talking, very fast and loud, emphatically and stiffly—he was active in student party affairs, and when he spoke to one man it was as if addressing millions. The shadows cast by his vigorous gestures ran back and forth across the ceiling. Franciszek did not hear him; he looked at him with half-closed eyes, and although Elzbieta was not in the room, he saw her pure and austere face beside Roman's. "So that's how it is," he thought. "This little black beetle, and you—so clear and pure. Your calm and his arrogance; he solves all your problems for you in a minute, problems you'd struggle with for weeks on end. He'll explain everything to you, and everything will come out even as in a multiplication table. He is your fool and your sorcerer; and you, my little one, you think you're in love with him. What do you look like together—this barking dwarf and you?"

"Elzbieta," he said, "I'm in a hurry."

After a while she came in carrying a tray with a steaming dish. "You and Mikołaj think that everything makes itself," she said. "Or that I have a dozen gnomes in the kitchen to help me."

"A dozen, no, but one . . ." Franciszek began, and bit his tongue. Whenever he recalled that Elzbieta was an adult, and that there were matters of life about which she need no longer consult him, he could not bear the sight of her and Roman together.

"What's that?"

"Nothing. It's hot. When is Mikołaj coming?"

She glanced at the clock. "He should be here now."

"He is always late."

"Always."

Franciszek knew that Mikołaj and Roman could not stand each other. Whenever he wanted to get rid of Roman, he talked about Mikołaj: the effect was instantaneous. This time it worked again. Roman began to move restlessly about the room; finally he said he had to leave and would be back tomorrow. He said a long goodbye to Elzbieta in the entrance hall, and managed to say "Bye-bye, Pop" several times. At last, to Franciszek's great relief, the door banged shut. Elzbieta came back into the room.

"I don't like him," he said.

She nodded. "I know."

"I'm sorry."

"So am I. But I'm sure you understand."

"I'm trying."

She smiled weakly. "You're wonderful."

"Will you tell me something frankly? As frankly as you can."

"I'll try."

"I want you to tell me, yes or no."

"Yes?"

"Do you love him?"

"You know that I do."

"Very much?"

"As much as I'm capable of."

"You're sure?"

Her clear eyes filled with light. He sighed.

"Yes," she said.

He wanted to question her about their relationship, but he suddenly felt ashamed. "Why do I have to talk to her about these things?" he thought angrily. "Am I afraid, or what? It's I who should tell her everything, not the other way around.

No, damn it, I must tell her at once ..." He put his fork down, and was about to tell her, but she spoke first.

"You've guessed everything, haven't you?"

"I've guessed what?"

She peered at him closely. "You know everything," she said.

He felt as if he had swallowed a lump of ice. He suddenly began to fear that she would tell him something that would merely sound bad; that she was too young to tell him everything clearly and well; and that she would use some unfortunate words that would torment him for years afterward. He said: "I know ... he is the only human being ..."

"Not the only one," she said. "Now there is a second one ..."

"Have you fallen in love with someone else?" He was about to jump from his chair when he saw her calm, almost victorious smile.

"Most of us love our own children," she said. He looked at her, and suddenly time vanished, the years opening up like the waters in fairy tales: his own wife had used the same words, and said them in the same way to announce that she was pregnant with Mikołaj.

"You know it for sure?"

"For sure."

"My little girl," he whispered. "But ..."

"There's something I never told you. He's very sick."

"Who?"

"Roman."

"Sick?"

"Consumption. I'm worried about him, Father. He's very depressed; this has been going on for months. He says he's going to die; he thinks about it all the time. He wants me to think of—him."

"And what does he say about this?"

"Nothing."

"How so?"

"He doesn't know."

"You didn't tell him?"

"I'll tell him when the time comes."

"You can tell him now. You've got to."

She shook her head. "I'm afraid to," she said. "He might want me to—he's sick, he'll be afraid. I'll tell him after it's . . ." She stopped.

"Why?" Franciszek whispered.

"I want them to live, both of them."

Franciszek turned away; Elzbieta walked quietly out of the room, carrying the dish. He drummed his fingers on the windowpane. On the floor above, someone was torturing a piano; the fingers of the invisible player kept stumbling on the same key. In the street a man with a long pole passed, lighting the lamps; the gleam of a newly lit lamp and the false note on the floor above came almost simultaneously.

"You look like an Italian woman praying to God and waiting for her husband. They stand by the window for hours, exactly as you're doing now."

He turned. "Did you buy a newspaper, Mikołaj?"

"Yes."

"Are you going somewhere tonight?"

"Have you something to tell me?"

"Yes."

"Just a minute, I want to wash my hands."

Mikołaj left the room. He was dangerously handsome; his face, voice, silhouette, the gleam in his eyes, his smile or grimace, his animal gait, his calm sleep, the manner in which he flipped away a cigarette butt—everything nature had given him was like a constant humiliation to others, a summons to hide their faces, to keep offstage, to stop talking, smiling, and breathing loudly. After a moment he came back and sat opposite Franciszek.

"Listen, Mikołaj," Franciszek said. "I've been expelled from the party."

"Are you drunk?"

"I'm sober. I haven't touched a drink."

"Then don't talk that way."

"It happened yesterday. I did something I can't understand. It seems like a nightmare. But it's a fact."

Mikołaj walked up to him and looked him in the eyes. Franciszek drew back, hunching up a little: his son was staring at him as if he were some strange thing. They were silent; Elzbieta was clattering dishes in the kitchen.

Mikołaj said at last: "Why?"

"It's my fault."

"What did you do?"

"Listen: I met a friend I hadn't seen since the days of the underground. We drank a few drinks. Then the police stopped me—two hard-boiled kids. I began to talk back to them—I was sober, damn it, suddenly quite sober; and they badgered me, they wanted to take me to the police station. In the end I flew into a rage, and I shouted things I can't remember. Next morning they told me what I had shouted, Mikołaj; I shouted that they could stick everything—you understand, everything—somewhere; that I didn't believe in anything; and I insulted the party, and . . ." He suddenly fell silent.

"Well?"

"Mikołaj, the fact is I don't think that way; you know it. I've never thought that way. I can't understand it."

"Then why did you shout?" Mikołaj asked tonelessly.

"I don't know. That's the worst of it."

"What happened then?"

"I wanted to get the matter cleared up right away. But I failed. That is to say, I was expelled. They have a record at the police station, you understand. Everything is written down, every word. There can't be any mistake. I must really have shouted those things."

"That means you think them."

"Mikołaj," Franciszek said imploringly, "surely you know me as well as a son can know a father. You have no right to speak like that."

"We aren't talking as father and son," Mikołaj said.

"No? As what, then?"

"As party comrade to party comrade."

"I don't think that way," he whispered. "You know I don't."

"You speak that way. You shout that way. Were you sober?"

"Yes."

"Are you sure?"

"As sure as I'm here. Maybe a bit edgy."

"So at other times—when you are sober as you are now—you also say things you don't feel?"

"No, no."

"And then what?"

"I don't understand. I don't understand it myself. Maybe it's a mistake?"

"Haven't you checked?"

"I have," Franciszek whispered. He passed his hand over his forehead. "In the morning when I was released they told me. And our secretary, too, checked . . . No, it's not a mistake. I must really have insulted the party."

"Yes, you must have."

"And I don't understand it."

"That you shouted?"

"It's a vicious circle of some kind. I shouted something I don't feel."

"And when you shout, 'Long live socialism, the party, Stalin,' don't you feel it either?"

"How can you?"

"How could you?"

"Mikołaj . . ."

Mikołaj got up. "There's no Mikołaj . . . You've been expelled from the party, haven't you?"

"Yes."

"For duplicity, yes?"

"Yes."

"Who is right—you or the party?"

"I."

"And who shouted?"

"I."

"So you weren't right. Whom shall I believe—you, an individual, you who shout something you don't feel, something you can't account for—or the party?"

"We must believe the party," Franciszek whispered.

"If that's so, we can't stay together," Mikołaj said.

"You want to leave home?"

Mikołaj did not reply. An hour went by. Franciszek watched Mikołaj pack his things in a valise—a modest suit of clothes, books, cheap shirts.

"You're really going," Franciszek said. He was silent a long while, then he added: "Who knows, maybe I'd do the same thing in your place."

"I'll come back after you've cleared yourself."

"What am I to do?"

"Stand up and fight. Maybe you'll find somebody, some

comrades, who'll believe you and be able to settle things for you. I've got to believe the party."

"And not me? I am your father; in spite of everything I am your father, whether you like it or not ... Can't you believe me?"

Mikołaj was already in his overcoat. He walked to the window; the light of the street lamp glinted in his hair.

"Believe—you? You alone? No." He turned round violently. "What do you know about the world, about how vile it is? You're still living in the past, in the underground—don't you realize what is going on today? Don't you really understand anything?" Once again he stared into the street. "If they tore the fronts off the houses, we'd see pigsties. I can't afford to believe any individual. I can only believe the party. If I didn't have the party to look up to, I'd become the vilest of the vile. I couldn't live otherwise. And you want me to believe you, you of all people—a shouter and a liar?"

"I am your father!" Franciszek cried.

Mikołaj smiled gloomily. "You are Franciszek Kowalski, expelled from the party for duplicity. The rest is beside the point, an accident. If the party takes you back, I'll apologize to you."

He picked up his valise. "Goodbye."

"Goodbye," Franciszek said after him. He stood by the window; he saw Mikołaj leave the house, and walk resolutely down the street. Then his son disappeared around a corner. Again trams, autos went by; over the slippery pavement, when it was empty for a moment, spread the red glow of the neon sign: YOUNG PEOPLE READ . . .—the only glow above the thick darkness of the city.

# X

THE STREET CAME ABRUPTLY TO AN END, AND
Franciszek stopped. Farther on there were fields, dilapidated
wooden buildings, unkempt yards, and smoking piles of rub-
bish; in the fields wrecked cars protruded from under the
thawing snow; the sun setting behind the distant city walls
gleamed red on their rusty bodies. Franciszek looked about
him helplessly—he had never before been in this section. Finally he stopped a passer-by. "I beg your pardon; can you
direct me to Acacia Street?"

"Over there."

"Where that tall house is?"

"Yes. I'm going that way myself."

They walked along a wet path, avoiding puddles. The
stranger asked: "Are you going to watch them clear the snow?"

"What are they doing?"

"They're clearing the snow."

"Where?"

"From the roof of that very house. My son told me, so I'm
going to watch."

True enough, before the tall building toward which they
waded through the slush stood a large throng of spectators,
craning their necks. On the roof a man with a shovel was
busily tossing piles of snow into the street; the object of the
game was to try to hit an unsuspecting passer-by. From a
distance they could hear the happy laughs and enthusiastic
shouts that greeted each heave of the shovel.

"I beg your pardon," the stranger said, tipping his cap. "I must drop in to see a friend, he'll be glad to ..." He scrutinized Franciszek's face. "Are you by chance from Bloc Committee No. 385?"

"Me? What gave you that idea?"

"I'm only asking. We're expecting a lecturer today, and, seeing that you're not from this neighborhood, I thought it might be you. He's going to lecture about the sun or something. They say we'll be getting electricity from the sun. Do you think that's possible?"

Franciszek was about to reply when a mad turmoil broke out before the tall house, and both he and his companion turned their heads. The man with the shovel had succeeded in dropping an avalanche of snow on the heads of three passing hunchbacks, who stood dazed, not knowing what had happened to them. The onlookers were delirious with joy; the man on the roof was shouting merrily, triumphantly waving his shovel.

"Is it possible?" the stranger asked thoughtfully.

"What?"

"That electricity business."

"Yes, certainly ... someday. Goodbye."

"Someday," the stranger repeated, and walked off. To the accompaniment of the happy clamor, Franciszek continued on his way until he found the house he had been looking for. It was an old tumbledown building; the wind was tearing at pieces of rotten tarpaper on the roof. Surprised by the squalor of the place, Franciszek stood staring for a few moments, then, with a shrug, plunged into the shadows as into dark water. He waded on blindly, groping for the wall—at last he touched its rough ratlike dampness, and drew back his hand in disgust. There was a smell of washing, of children; from an upper floor came the echoes of a quarrel. He struck a match, and looked for the number by the light of its uncertain flame. At last he stopped at a door, and knocked.

No one answered; a woman was shouting loudly on the same floor. Franciszek was about to leave when he thought he heard a rustling noise behind the door. He knocked again, and then again, louder; at last he heard the sound of shuffling feet.

"Who is it?" a woman's voice asked.

"Is Mr. Zakrzewski at home?"

There was a moment's silence. "What's your business?"

"I want to see him."

"And who are you?"

"Kowalski."

There was another brief silence. "Wait a minute," the woman said.

He lighted a cigarette; behind the door the sound of shuffling feet receded. From the street came a roar of rage and a triumphant clamor; once again a shovelful of snow had found its mark. The bolt creaked in the door.

"Come in," the woman said.

He crossed a small passageway, and entered a room. Behind a table a giant of a man rose from his seat; he was so huge that the time it took him to lift his powerful bulk seemed infinitely long. "You wanted to see me?" he asked.

Franciszek was silent, looking him straight in the eyes. Then he said softly: "Bear—don't you recognize me?"

"I'm sorry," the man stammered. "But ... my name is Zakrzewski, Wacław Zakrzewski. I'll ... show you ... my identity card."

"Bear," Franciszek repeated, "is it possible you don't recognize me? I am Kowalski, Franciszek—'Skinny'—have you forgotten everything? We fought together in the underground."

For a long while they regarded each other in silence. The enormous man sat down heavily. "I knew you'd find me someday," he said in a low voice. "Well, here I am. There's nothing in life that can be wiped out, nothing can be forgotten . . ." He raised his head. "May I say goodbye to my wife?"

Franciszek stepped back. "You're out of your mind," he said. "What makes you think I'm from the secret police? I just wanted to see you, to find out how you were, to talk to you . . ." He walked up to him and held out his hand. Bear swerved violently. "Bear," Franciszek said, looking with horror at his face, which had turned white, "what's happened to you? Why do I find you like this? Bear . . ."

"Shh, quiet!" Bear hissed. "Don't call me by that name. What do you want?"

Franciszek sat down, his hat in his hands. "So this is what you've come to," he said thoughtfully. "Twelve years in Bereza prison before the war for being a Communist; a price put on your head by the Germans; songs written about you in the underground . . ." He passed his hand over his forehead. "My God," he whispered, "where am I? Is it a dream? Is it real?" Once again he looked at the other's huge dead face. He shook his head, and suddenly burst out laughing. "I remember you," he cried; "I remember that I wanted to be like you; I remember that we were proud of you; I remember the day you were decorated; how we drank home-brew to the health of your medals—Jerzy, myself, everyone else . . ." He paused, and then asked dully: "What's happened to you, Bear?"

"Shh, quiet!" Bear hissed. "Just a minute."

He violently turned the handle of a phonograph and put on a record. A rasping voice came through the horn:

"And Jozio came and brought the doughnuts,
And kissed her hands, and kissed her hands ..."

"What did you come for?" Bear asked.

"I've made up my mind to look up my comrades in the underground," Franciszek said. "I remembered the names of the best among them and got their addresses. I must look them up and ask them to help me ... You know me; you know what it was like in the underground," he said imploringly. "You know how I talked, how I thought, how I behaved. I need help, Bear. I slipped, though it's difficult to call it a slip. In short, what I want is—" He broke off; it was hard for him to collect his thoughts. He looked at Bear, expecting him somehow to come to his aid, but Bear remained silent, staring at the floor. The phonograph scratched on:

"And Jozio came and brought the doughnuts,
And kissed her hands, and kissed her hands ..."

"One day I got drunk," Franciszek said, "and I talked foolishly. At first the whole thing seemed trivial to me, but I know I said that I did not trust our leaders, that I had no faith in the party, and I told them to stick it all up somewhere. What I want is to get my old comrades to—well—to speak for me. If need be I'll go to the boss himself, but I am interested in finding people who would be willing to say something in my behalf. After all, I don't think that way, and I said all that when I was drunk. Surely you remember me. Will you help me, Bear?"

"Just a minute," said Bear. He turned off the phonograph. "This music is no good," he said. "There are people all around;

someone may be listening in." He jumped up from his seat, rushed to the other room, and after a moment came back with a little boy. "This is my son," he said to Franciszek, and made the boy stand in a corner with his face to the wall. "Recite Mayakovsky," he said, and the boy began to declaim in a monotonous voice, staring with round eyes at the empty wall. "Now go on with your story," Bear said to Franciszek.

"I was expelled from the party," Franciszek said. "My case will go to the District Committee, perhaps to the executive of the Regional Committee. Tell me, Bear, was I ever ..." He wanted to say "twofaced," but he suddenly realized how ridiculous he was: what did they know about each other, he and the man facing him? He stared gloomily at Bear. Now one thing was clear to him: he was guilty. He must have done something that estranged him from the party, that estranged him even from Mikołaj; now that something was closing the mouth of this man. The thought of his guilt almost brought him relief. "Yes," he said in a low voice, "I did something terrible, I know it's terrible, and I don't myself understand how it could have happened. But can one moment, in which a man is not accountable for his thoughts and words, wipe out his whole life and everything he has done? Is there really such a crime?"

Again he fell silent. The boy went on reciting in a voice as monotonous as the dripping of water from a spout:

"Beyond the mountains of defeats the dawns glow,
A new sunlit country is awaiting us.
Against starvation, against the sea of pestilence
Our million steps resound.
Though a mercenary gang surrounds us ..."

"Will you help me, Bear?" Franciszek asked.

"Have you been to see anyone else?"

"No, I just telephoned Jerzy. I was told that he was on vacation, and that he'd be back in a few days. I looked you up first . . ." He took his hand. "You won't refuse me, will you?"

"Now sing, Franek," Bear said to the boy, who began at once, "On the Vistula, the broad Vistula, rose the builders' song . . ." Bear said to Franciszek: "I named him after you, in memory of those days. How can I help you?"

"I beg your pardon," Franciszek said, annoyed. "This is very nice of you, but must the child sing? Must he be present during our talk? Who the devil is listening in here, and what for?"

"No, that's not it," Bear stammered, "but you know, silence is no good either, so let him sing; he likes it, anyway. When it's too silent, your neighbors think at once, 'Aha, they're plotting something; why should anybody live so quietly?' And they begin to have foolish ideas, about spies, or enemies. Why, sometimes I have fights with my wife, just so as not to seem too quiet. Let him sing. But if it bothers you, he can recite poetry. Franek, recite 'Vladimir Ilyich.'"

Franek began at once to declaim in the same bored tone:

"The party is the backbone of our class,
The party is our immortal cause,
The party, the one thing that won't betray me;
Today I am a subject, tomorrow I abolish empires.
The brain of the class, the cause of the class . . ."

"So what do you want?" Bear asked.

"I want you to help me. You, a former partisan, an officer. Don't you understand? You are Bear, aren't you?"

"No," said Bear. "And I refuse even to remember it. Or to talk about it. Or to think about it. Do you understand?"

"So you've cut all that out of your past?" Franciszek asked. "You, a legendary partisan, a hero, the pride of your unit ... you've cut all that out. Is that true?"

They measured each other.

"It's true," Bear said.

"Don't turn around, Franek," Franciszek said to the boy. And, while the child went on reciting, he walked up to Bear and slapped him in the face.

He walked out. Was that really water dripping—or was it Bear's little boy still talking and staring with his black eyes at the murky grayness of the wall? He was in the street when Bear caught up with him. They walked side by side in silence, breathing heavily.

"Listen," Bear stammered. He gripped Franciszek's arm and looked in his eyes, stumbling all the while. "It isn't the way you think it is. Listen, you've got to understand. I have a son ..."

"Franek," Franciszek said. "In memory of those moments."

"Those moments, those moments," Bear stammered. "What are they next to life? Next to the fear you've got to live with, constantly, without interruption, from morning till night? Can we bask in the days of glory when we live in a time of pestilence? They'll finish us off, you, me, Jerzy. Our time is over; and the others, the ones on top, they know it. They commit crimes when they have to, but in spite of everything they're laying the foundations for faith in man; they believe in you, in me, in Jerzy, and that's why they'll finish us off when the time comes. They believe that we're somehow decent, and that someday we'll wake up, and let out a wild shout: no! And maybe this shout will be taken up by a few others. It's

neither you nor I that's at stake, but something beside which
we mean nothing at all. Ah, Franciszek, we wanted to take the
road to life, and we've come to a graveyard; we set out for a
promised land, and all we see is a desert; we talked about justice, and all we know is terror and despair. Once I lived on the
fourth floor, and all day long I did nothing but count people's
footsteps on the staircase—were they coming for me or not?
Someday they would come, I thought. History has no use for
witnesses. The next generation will rush headlong into whatever is expected of it. It will regard each of the crimes now
being committed as sacred, as necessary. And what about
us? You? Me? We've done our part, and now we must try to
survive, just survive as long as possible. Do you want to be
the righteous man of Gomorrah? What do you want? Testi-
monials? Give it up. Can't you die like a strong animal, alone
and in silence? You've nothing left, no teeth to bite with, and
nothing to shoot with. Go away, and if you don't understand,
at least leave the rest of us alone. After all, we're entitled to
something in return for our days of glory; at least we have the
right to be forgotten."

"Have you seen Jerzy since those days?" Franciszek asked.

"No, and I don't want to see him."

Franciszek slackened his pace. "You certainly don't think,"
he said, "that he would ever be capable of saying the kind of
thing you've just said. Do you?"

They were silent for a while.

"No," Bear said. "Jerzy? No, Jerzy will never say such
things, I know. I often think of him; he was the purest of all,
better than either of us. Maybe that's what has saved him."

They stopped.

"Farewell, Bear," Franciszek said.

"Goodbye, Skinny," Bear said.

Neither of them saw the other's face: they were far from any street lamp, standing in darkness and rain. After a moment's hesitation, each of them extended a hand. Their hands did not meet, but they pretended not to notice.

# XI

STILL WEARING HIS OVERCOAT, HE WALKED INTO his living room. "Why don't you turn on the light, Elzbieta?" he asked. He walked up to her and saw her face was drenched with tears. "Something bad happened to you, my little girl?"

She tried to smile. "No, no."

He sat down beside her. "Then why are you crying?"

"Really, it's nothing."

"Something unpleasant?"

"Yes," she said, and began to sob. "At school."

"What was it?"

She opened her mouth, but he saw that she was making up an answer. "I don't know why," she said, staring over his head, "but the instructor picks on me all the time."

"And why isn't Roman with you?"

Once again she raised her face. "He's very busy now," she said. "You know it will soon be May Day."

"Yes," he said. He walked to the window and rested his burning head against the cold glass. "Don't let my troubles upset you, Elzbieta. I'll manage somehow. I'll look up my former companions; they'll help me."

He gazed at the hysterical quivering of the neon sign and thought: "And yet I must have done something. Somewhere inside me there must be some doubt I wasn't aware of; it rose to the surface at the first opportunity, in a moment of exhaustion. What was it I doubted? The party? The people? The leadership? Or could it be the cause? How strong a man must be to go through life with a clear head, ignoring doubts, fears, sordid thoughts! What would I have been if I had no faith in the cause, if it had not been my goal, if it were not my goal even now, my brightest star? Bear? A madman. What did Mikołaj say? Stand up and fight. Very well, I will." He was strong again. It seemed to him that from the silent city, from the calm sky, from the streets below and the stars above, faith invaded him, effacing all his trials, and that this faith would endure in him as long as the earth turned around the sun.

"Good night, Elzbieta," he said.

# XII

HE WAS ABOUT TO LEAVE THE FACTORY: THE SIRENS were wailing. He punched his timecard and was walking toward the gate, when the porter stopped him. "I have a little note for you," he said in a strangely official tone, without his usual wink. He took out his receipt book, and slowly moved his trembling finger over the page, looking for the place. "Oh, here it is," he said finally. "Please, sign here."

Franciszek signed and walked out. In the street he stopped to read the note. The Personnel Department was notifying him that his employment would be terminated in three months; during that time he would have to look for another job and another apartment.

"Hey, Citizen!" someone cried behind him.

He turned around. Jarzebowski was running toward him, his overcoat unbuttoned, his hair flying in the wind.

"Well?" he shouted from a distance. "Well, how about it?"

"What do you mean?"

"You don't know? Our glee club. You're gifted, you know; there's no doubt that you have a real talent . . ."

Franciszek smiled and walked away. He stared at the crumbling wet sidewalks, thinking: "Aren't they right? They don't trust me and they don't want me—it's simple." At this moment he was proud of his party, of the men who had expelled him; he was proud of their logic, inflexibility, purity; he was proud of his son, Mikołaj. And he thought happily that had he been in their place he would have acted as they did. Stand up and fight, return to them pure, and deserving to be trusted—that was what he had to do.

The sidewalk ended suddenly at a long red wall; he was walking across an empty square, full of mud. Somewhere at the end of it a group of people had gathered, murmuring joyfully; he could also hear the barking of a dog—undoubtedly a very big dog. He walked up to them without thinking, and elbowed his way through the ring of bystanders. The object of their curiosity was a man in a fencing mask and gauntlets, who was pulling a beautiful dog by a chain, addressing it with horrible curses. It was obvious that the beautiful dog was quite unimpressed by the curses. Franciszek thought at first that the strangely dressed man was some sort of trainer, and was about to turn away, when the man suddenly removed his mask with a tired gesture, and Franciszek saw before him the frantic eyes of Comrade Nowak.

"Nowak," he cried in surprise. "What the devil are you doing here?"

Nowak wiped the sweat from his forehead. "Ah, it's you," he said in a wooden voice. "Have you got a cigarette? I'm exhausted..."

"What are you doing with that dog?"

"The dog?" asked Nowak, staring vacantly. He had a bitter smile. "True, for you it may be only a dog, but for me..." He suddenly raised his fists to the sky, and howled: "For me it's worse than a hyena, worse than leprosy." He jerked the chain, but the dog did not even budge. "Red, you damn' beast," Nowak cried, "stand up! Stand up, I say!"

The crowd around them laughed happily. The beautiful dog sat motionless, staring haughtily out of its bronze-colored eyes.

"Red," Nowak whispered. He lurched as he raised his right hand in a dramatic gesture. "Red, I implore you . . . Red, my precious, stand up, please . . ."

"For God's sake," said Franciszek angrily, "what do you want of this dog?"

"What do you mean?" Nowak asked. "You yourselves ordered me to change his name!" He moved closer to Franciszek. "He used to be called Sambo, and everything was fine," he whispered passionately. "A real jewel, not a dog: he brought me the newspaper in his mouth; he loved the children; he walked my little girl home from school; he looked after a blind old man from across the street; and so on . . . But ever since the party secretary ordered me to call him Red— you remember, don't you?—his character has changed. He attacks everybody; he snaps; my wife is leaving me; she can't get along with him. She's already seen a lawyer . . ." He sighed. "All because of the dog. Of course, this won't be mentioned in court; we mustn't compromise the party . . ." He gritted his teeth. "We've decided she will say I didn't satisfy her sexually, and that she believes in free love. Of course, we'll keep seeing each other somehow. But we can't do it any other way without compromising the party; we can't. There's no other way, really there isn't. I've thought it over very carefully."

"But can't you get rid of the dog?"

"Get rid of him?" Nowak repeated, suddenly amused, and looked at Franciszek as if he were a kind of imbecile. "Get rid of him? I tried to drown him; I gave him a pound of rat poison a day; I turned on the radio full blast and left my family for three days; I took him a hundred miles from Warsaw, and he came back. But I can't sell him with the name Sambo— that would be like giving arms to the enemy. No, I can't get rid of him: the Michurin-Pavlov Society would get after me in a second— What have you done with your dog? Why do you mistreat animals? Don't you realize what a dog can do for a man, particularly for a party comrade? . . ." He resolutely put on his mask. "Excuse me," he said, "but I've got to get to work. This is my party assignment; for this purpose I was released from participation in the city-to-village campaign." He jerked the chain desperately. "Come on, Red," he cried. "Stand up!"

The dog pricked up one ear, then lay down on its belly, stretching out its two aristocratic forelegs: he looked like a fur rug. Jerks, curses, caresses, promises—nothing helped. Nowak toiled and sweated, the crowd roared happily, and amid this commotion only the dog remained noble and calm.

"What's going on here?" a brisk voice cried suddenly. A young policeman forced his way through the crowd. "What's this?" He turned to the nearest spectator and looked him sternly in the eyes. "Is there something you don't like? Now tell the truth: you don't like the regime?"

"Mr. Authority," said the other. "I'm leaving. I've already left. I've never been here."

He tipped his hat, and vanished. Reluctantly the crowd began to disperse. Only Franciszek, Nowak, the policeman, and the dog, who was exquisitely licking his paw, remained on the square.

"What are you up to?" the policeman asked Nowak. "What's the matter with you? Is it a joke or what? I see you don't like it here. If so, better say so, right away."

"I'm training a dog," Nowak replied haughtily. He removed his mask and fanned his flushed face. "If you don't believe me, there"—he pointed—"there's my factory, and you can find out all about me. I'm training the dog on the secretary's orders."

They stared at each other.

"What are you teaching it?" the policeman asked.

"Attitude," Nowak said dryly. "An attitude befitting a dog."

Again they exchanged stares.

"If that's the case," the policeman said, "everything is in order." He turned violently to Franciszek. "And what are you doing here, Citizen?" he asked sharply. "Maybe you . . ."

"I like it here," Franciszek said. "Everything is just as it should be." Nowak had gone away dragging his dog as a towman pulls his barge; Franciszek and the policeman looked at each other in silence. Suddenly Franciszek smiled. "Do you remember me?" he asked. "Surely you remember me."

The policeman moved a step forward, and his face lit up. "Why of course," he cried in a happy clear voice. "Of course I remember. I hooked you, didn't I, for disturbing the peace . . ." He was as happy as a child who has just been given a beautiful toy, and patted Franciszek on the arm. "Yes, yes," he repeated, his eyes sparkling, "It was you who disturbed the peace."

"Well," said Franciszek, smiling gloomily, "you might call it that."

"Why?" said the policeman, and his face suddenly clouded. "Don't you like the name?"

"Nonsense; I haven't said anything of the kind."

"And you're very pleased about it, aren't you?"

"What am I pleased about?"

"The fact that you haven't said anything of the kind. Admit it."

They were walking slowly across the deserted square. "Ah, my friend," Franciszek said, "if you had gone through what I have, you'd realize that that isn't enough: you like it, you don't like it. I raised my hand against things which neither conscience nor reason can grasp, which are beyond human

understanding. I know, I know it perfectly; I told you then
that there were no such things. I told you—it's a fact, I know
I told you—that everything described as beyond human understanding is at bottom an absurdity and a lie, and a crime
as well, and that it is not beyond man, but against man. That's
what I said, yes. I said that every human action can be measured only by a man's endurance and life, and by the amount
of happiness it gives him—however little. Yes, that's what I
said. What of it? Like everybody else, I had my moments of
doubt. My dear man: the more moments of doubt that can be
mastered by reason, the stronger the faith."

He turned to the policeman, but he was walking alone—
there was no one beside him. Somewhere near a fence three
old women stood gossiping, and the young policeman was
running toward them, holding up his long coat. A moment
later Franciszek could hear his resounding voice: "Do you
like it or don't you?" and the frightened chirping of the three
old women.

He entered a telephone booth and dialed a number. After
a while he heard the click of the receiver at the other end.
"Excuse me," he said; "may I speak to Jerzy?"

"Who is it?" a woman's voice asked.

"My name is Kowalski."

There was a moment's silence.

"Jerzy isn't in," the woman said. "Didn't you know?"

"No, I didn't."

Again the receiver was silent for a moment. Someone
knocked sharply at the booth window.

"On vacation," said the voice in the receiver. "You understand—on va-ca-tion. Surely he is entitled to a vacation,
isn't he?"

Franciszek wanted to say something, but the receiver

clicked at the other end. Again he was walking through the dark, empty city, which had been washed by rain for many weeks, and still refused to awaken to spring, the city with one neon sign over it: YOUNG PEOPLE READ *THE BANNER OF YO  H*." At home, he sat by the window in a cold draft; he looked at the blinking letters, and it seemed to him that over the noise and bustle of the city he could hear a sharp barking voice: "Do you like it or don't you? Do you like it or don't you? Do you like it or . . ."

Suddenly he turned around. "Why don't you serve supper, Elzbieta?"

He heard her stand up heavily and move off to the kitchen. He followed her. "You've broken with Roman, haven't you?"

She leaned on his arm and suddenly burst into tears.

"It will pass," he said, stroking her cold, heavy hair. "Everything will pass, my child. Everything evil, stupid, inhuman. We must think that we are continually moving toward light; we must believe in it . . ." He fell silent, and stared at the darkness outside and the quivering neon letters, and once again—against his will—read them from beginning to end, mentally replacing the missing ones. Then he pushed Elzbieta away, and violently drew the curtain, so violently that some of its rings tore off.

# XIII

HE STOPPED IN FRONT OF A TALL WHITE HOUSE, and checked the address on a slip of paper. He walked in, and was starting to climb the broad staircase when someone called from behind, "Hey, Citizen!"

He turned around, his hand on the banister: a soldier with a tommy gun slung over his shoulder stood on the landing below.

"Who do you want to see?" he asked Franciszek.

"A friend."

"What's this?" the soldier said, and his young face was suddenly clouded. "Without a pass? Come back down, Citizen." He held out his hand. "Your papers."

He slowly made out a pass for him on a red form, wetting his pencil and murmuring solemnly the while; finally he gave Franciszek his identification with the pass, and said, "Third floor." Then, as Franciszek was beginning to climb, he added in a chiding tone, "Next time, Citizen, don't try to get in without a pass."

He stopped at the third floor and rang the bell. The door opened for him, there were whispers, and finally he stood before the man he had come to see. "Do you recognize me, Birch?" Franciszek asked.

The man standing before him, with a sickly face and sunken, lusterless black eyes, scrutinized him carefully.

"Skinny," he said at last, holding out his hand. "It's Skinny, isn't it?"

"Yes," said Franciszek. "It's me."

They sat in armchairs. They looked at each other, trying to discover changes in one another's faces and gestures; for a few moments an awkward silence prevailed. Then Franciszek, trying to hide his embarrassment, began to speak hurriedly: "You must excuse me for bothering you—I know people like you have no time even for their families, but my case ..." He suddenly hesitated.

"Go on," Birch said. "I'm listening."

"Do you remember me as I was in the underground?"

"Yes, you, and the others too."

"Will you help me?"

"Surely that goes without saying," Birch said. "Talk."

"I ... I ..." Franciszek said, trying to look the other straight in the eyes, "I raised my hand against the party. I don't understand myself how it happened ..." He turned scarlet. "You know, I was a bit tight, and I shouted that ..."

He paused, suddenly overcome with a feeling that this talk was hopeless. "What did I shout?" he thought desperately, "What did I shout? After all, I said the truth, what I felt ..." He went on: "I said that I didn't believe that—that—"

"That what?"

"That it was possible to build anything valuable by means of crimes and lies, by destroying human dignity, by transforming Communist loyalty into slavery."

"And what am I to do about it?"

"I want you—you, one of the men who have power and know the authorities—I want you to tell me: Where is the dividing line between loyalty and slavery, between crime and necessity? It was always reason that drew that line, reason and conscience. And now—that's what I said then—now man has become only a miserable plaything of politics. We try to forget reason if we know what's good for us; and as for conscience, that miserable thing, it's better to think it never existed."

"Whom did you say all this to?"

"To whom? To whom? Does it matter? What matters is that I'm saying it to myself."

"What happened afterward?"

"What happened afterward is beside the point. I was expelled from the party. But that's beside the point too."

"And so?"

"I want you to tell me."

"Tell you what?"

"That I'm wrong."

They were silent for a while. The other looked at Franciszek with his lusterless eyes, his head slightly bowed. "Listen," he said at last. "The first year after the war I worked for the security police. I had a son; all through the occupation he was in the underground; then he took part in armed attacks, was riddled with bullets, lost one lung, and finally, as an invalid, he landed in my office. In my office, where he had to do the work of three strong healthy men. So he worked— interrogations, investigations, spies, saboteurs, diversionists. Once he questioned a diversionist; he had been questioning him I don't know how many nights on end; the prisoner behaved provocatively, and finally my boy—sick, almost dead with exhaustion, his nerves strained to the breaking point— couldn't stand it any more and struck the diversionist in the face." He paused.

"Well, what then?" Franciszek asked.

Birch smiled strangely. "Well, nothing," he said. "I had

to lock him up—eight years in jail. I myself saw to it that he was sentenced. And do you know what the diversionist got? Five years. He was a halfwit; he didn't even know what he was doing, or who he was working against. Whereas my son was a conscious, militant party member, and was supposed to know what he was doing."

He rose suddenly and began to pace the room. His neck grew purple, and his upper lip quivered. "Goddam it to hell!" he said. "To hell with this goddam chatter! What matters are the consequences, the final consequences. Once you've started a revolution, you have to realize that it can't be stopped, or moderated, or turned off, or delayed. A revolution can be only won or lost, and that's all. What horrifies you? The dimensions? The methods?"

"The consequences," Franciszek said. "What you said a moment ago. Is the revolution a blind, brutal force?"

Birch gripped Franciszek by the arm and led him to the window. Before them lay the wet city, bristling with scaffoldings. "Here, to this place," Birch said, "in I don't know how many years, a man will come who hasn't yet been born. He will come and he'll want to live, to have food, an apartment, children, a family; he will want to live in security and he will expect the time he lives in to provide everything a man is entitled to. I assure you that he won't be concerned with your sufferings and doubts, or mine. He will evaluate the world he finds by the yardstick of his reason. And that's all."

He fell silent. He looked down at the wet scaffoldings, and his sickly yellow face darkened.

"You have a son," Franciszek said. "I didn't know."

Birch raised his head. "'Have'?" he said. "I had. He's so sick he'll never survive it all ..." He walked up to the radio and turned the knob. "Excuse me, Franciszek," he said, "but yesterday I made a speech at a meeting and now they're going to broadcast it. I want to listen."

Franciszek was silent. What had he come here for? Who had he been talking to? And what had he expected to hear in reply? He had heard only what he himself had repeated a million times to himself and others, in order to find strength to act. And where was that strength? In Mikołaj's departure, in Bear's failure, or in the tired voice of this man who had sentenced his own son? Where was the goal, and the hope? Was it really in this man still unborn who would confront life unseeing, ignorant of the sacrifices and renunciations and defeats others had suffered for his sake, those others who had been tortured to death and thrown on the dung pile? If this contented blind man of the future, who would walk with a smile upon this filthy earth, was to be our hope, if our sacrifices were for his sake, what would justify them?

"May Day is near," Birch's voice said on the radio. "Comrades. The founders of Marxism-Leninism teach us that the working class cannot emancipate itself without emancipating all the oppressed and exploited, without abolishing all oppression and exploitation of man by man. The working class is the class under whose leadership mankind emancipates itself from all forms of social injustice, from everything that obstructs social progress. The working class is the class under whose leadership mankind takes the historic leap from the realm of necessity to the realm of freedom, achieves mastery over nature, and begins, through knowledge of the laws of social evolution, consciously to shape its fate."

He was interrupted by long and frantic applause. Then he went on:

"The doctrine of Marx and Engels was further developed by Lenin and Stalin, our Great Teacher. They developed it in the age of imperialism, when capitalist oppression and exploitation had spread over the entire terrestrial globe and combined with all the pre-capitalist forms of enslavement of labor, when the greed of the imperialist exploiters threw mankind into bloody wars of historically unprecedented dimensions, when the bourgeoisie and its ideologists betrayed and trampled upon all ideals, including the limited freedom and justice they themselves had once proclaimed, and when the working masses of the entire world were filled with a growing and irresistible aspiration for full social justice and full freedom—the aspiration toward socialism . . ."

Long and frantic applause.

"Lenin and the Great Teacher," the speaker went on, "developed the doctrine of Marx and Engels according to which the working class is the class destined to free mankind from all exploitation and oppression, and gave us the doctrine of the leadership of the proletariat in the struggles for national liberation, in the struggles of the peasant masses against the feudal regime and its survivals, in the struggles of all toiling people against the capitalist regime . . ."

Again there was a mighty clamor. "Long, resounding applause," Franciszek said. "That's what all the newspapers will say."

The speaker went on: "Standing at the head of all the oppressed and exploited in the struggle to overthrow imperialist tyranny, forging the alliance between the workers and the toiling peasants and the popular masses engaged in a struggle for national liberation, the party of the proletariat raises the banner of emancipation in the name of the overwhelming majority of society against an insignificant minority of exploiters. The leadership of the working class aims at carrying out, by the proletariat, a great revolutionary task, consisting in the creation of new social conditions in the interests of the overwhelming majority of people in the whole world, and in the construction of a socialist society . . ."

"Everything true to form," Franciszek said, "wasn't it? The hired orphan with the flowers, and some old fogy, a veteran of the 1905 revolution, whom you embraced before the cameras; and secret policemen in dark blue uniforms behind you. Wasn't it so?"

"Correct," said Birch. "And there were people who, after the whole thing was over, asked whether I couldn't get the woman at the refreshment stand to open an hour early; and there was a fellow who whispered into my ear, 'Malinowski is a thief.' "

"But these details won't be broadcast, will they?" Franciszek said.

"No, they won't," said Birch.

He fell silent and listened to his own voice: "The victorious Great Socialist October Revolution created the first proletarian state, the Soviet state. Henceforward, loyalty to proletarian internationalism is above all loyalty to October. It is no accident that the treachery of the Tito clique manifested itself from the outset in its anti-Soviet attitude, in its negation of the leading role of the Soviet Union. It is no accident that anti-Soviet tendencies were at the basis of Gomułkism, the Polish variety of Titoism. The great achievement of the Soviet Union is the model, the example, the hope of the world. It is a model which proves that there is a way out of depressions and misery, economic and cultural backwardness, oppressions of national minorities, and wars between nations. It is an example which teaches us how to overthrow the rule of capitalists and landlords, how to build a new, just society. It is the hope of all those who are oppressed by exploiters, enslaved by imperialists, tortured by reactionaries who hate the toiling masses. The great constructive work of the Soviet Union is a source of strength for the proletarian movement, for progressive and libertarian movements the world over. It is the strength of the Soviet Union that smashed the Hitlerite dream of making a fascist master race the rulers of the world. It is the strength of the Soviet Union that stands in the way of the Wall Street magnates who are trying to repeat Hitler's attempt to enslave mankind. The international proletariat led by the Soviet Union has become the vanguard of mankind, of all toiling men, of all the oppressed and exploited the world over, in the struggle for a better tomorrow without wars, a tomorrow without oppression and exploitation, a tomorrow of material prosperity and cultural flowering . . ." His voice was drowned out for a while; once again there was a clamor in the great auditorium, and happy cries rang out; at one point someone could even be heard saying, "There was misery, there was capitalism; then came a man named Lenin . . ."

"And now long, frantic applause," Franciszek said. "How absurd!"

"What?"

"How you must despise these people, hate these poor ants, this working class, these people who have the leadership. On the one hand you have to keep flattering them to get a spark of effort out of them; on the other hand, you have to force them to do things which surely seem inhuman even to yourself." He rose and walked to the window. "And yet there will surely come a time when you will have to stop talking about leadership and look them in the face," he said. "And what will you see then? What people? The results will be beyond your expectation . . ." He returned to his armchair. "The only comforting thought is that you have no longer anything in common with any class, or with any people," he said. "If there is such a thing as comfort."

The applause died gradually, and again Birch's voice resounded from the loudspeaker: "May Day is near, the holiday of the workers' struggle, the holiday of proletarian internationalism, the holiday of the international solidarity of the proletariat. We shall celebrate this May Day at a moment when each passing hour witnesses new reports of the peaceful victories of the construction of Communism in the great Soviet Union, the state of victorious socialism, the hope of toiling mankind ..." A last great storm of applause; then the noise gradually subsided, and the announcer promised a symphony concert. Franciszek and Birch exchanged glances.

"And then," Birch said, "after long, endless applause, I went out into the yard, in front of the factory. The man you asked me about, the old fogy, veteran of the 1905 revolution, stepped up to me. He works in the factory as a night watchman; he asked if I couldn't get him transferred to the position of a dog. 'What do you mean—a dog?' I asked. 'Ah,' he said, 'the appropriation for a night watchman is a little over four hundred złotys, and almost six hundred is paid for the upkeep of the dog. So you see, comrade, maybe I could change places with the dog. I won't starve the animal, my word of honor as a worker, but my own position will improve and no one will be the loser.' Well, Franciszek? Shall we laugh, or start firing guns?" He rose and paced the floor; then he stopped in front of Franciszek. "Memory," he said. "That's our only shield against doubts. We must constantly remember where we come from."

"Have you forgotten?"

"Have I forgotten what?"

"It's very funny," Franciszek said, "and I often laugh at it myself, but the only sense in any action is man, and his short, sad life: unfortunately there's nothing we can do about it, no matter how hard we might try. Apparently that's how it has to be; in this accursed world, man, little as he is, has to be a giant; and in the actual relationship of forces, everything else is tiny—the great construction projects, the dams, the canals, the Dneprostroi, and God knows what. Unfortunately you can't turn all this upside down."

"What have you come for, Franciszek?" Birch asked. "For faith?"

"Yes," Franciszek replied seriously, "for faith."

"So you have no faith?"

"I have faith," Franciszek said, "but not in you any more. I believe in Communism, if it can be saved from you, and if you quit in time. Pieces of wreckage can't guide anyone lost at sea . . ." He paused, and then whispered, "Jerzy, perhaps."

He saw Birch's face give a sudden twitch. "What about Jerzy?" he asked sharply.

"He must be different."

"Jerzy," Birch said, smiling. "Yes, you're right; go to see him. He is different. Even more different than you think."

"Do you remember him?"

"Very well indeed."

"Yes," Franciszek said, shaking his head stubbornly. "He must be different. Different—from all of us."

"Go to see him," Birch said. "I can do only one thing for you: after you leave I can try to think that we chatted about the good old simple times in the underground."

Franciszek rose.

"I can give you a lift," Birch said. "I'm about to leave myself."

"Where are you going? In what direction?"

"To the big electrical machine plant."

"To a meeting?"

"Yes."

"You'll make a speech?"

"Yes."

"About the leadership of the working class?"

"Yes."

He held out his hand; and both pretended not to notice that their hands avoided each other.

"Goodbye, Birch," Franciszek said.

"Goodbye, Skinny," Birch said.

Again he walked through the nighttime city, wading in the wet, filthy snow; there was still not even the slightest sign of spring. Wherever he looked, he saw nothing but mud, patches of snow thawing in black puddles, and trash drifting about the pavements; nothing but the clammy darkness over which the single neon sign quivered hysterically. "Jerzy; of course, Jerzy," Franciszek thought. "He is different, purer and better. Surely he's putting up a fight, and he knows how to fight; it's his destiny to fight this vile thing." There was a telephone booth at the corner, and he hurried toward it. He waited a long time outside the glass door; someone with his back turned to him was talking vehemently, gesticulating madly with his left hand, in a strangely familiar way. Finally he hung up the receiver, and walked out.

"Roman," Franciszek said with surprise. "Good evening."

He held out his hand. His daughter's fiancé stopped and looked sharply in his face. His childish mouth curled in contempt. Without a word, he turned and walked off, whistling shrilly. Franciszek stood motionless for a long time, numb with fury and astonishment; finally he walked in and dialed his number. After a while he heard the same woman's voice.

"May I speak to Jerzy?" he asked.

"Who is it?"

"Please tell him it's Franciszek. Or better still: Skinny."

For a moment the receiver was silent. A stoutish man outside began to bang the glass door with the handle of his umbrella. Then the woman said: "Jerzy is on vacation. Do you get me? On va-ca-tion."

# XIV

HE WALKED DOWN A DARK CORRIDOR, STUMBLING over empty milk bottles and pieces of junk that had lain there for years; he trampled on innumerable dogs and cats and groped in the darkness and clouds of dust. Here and there the darkness was broken by the light bulbs protected by wire nets. Their dim glow, the smell of dust, the screaming of the cats, the smell of washing, and the fumes of cabbage cooking on every floor from the basement to the attic made Franciszek's head ache. This was an old house; it had been hit by a bomb which had opened up a terrible gash in its left wing; the staircase broke off abruptly, and one could see the wet street below, the slippery sidewalks, and the hurrying pedestrians. Franciszek stopped.

"Uncle, Uncle, please unchain me," a thin little voice said.

He turned. In the corridor, a little boy was sitting on the floor, attached to the banister by an iron chain fastened with a padlock.

"Who chained you?" Franciszek said.

"Mama," said the boy.

"Mama? Why?"

"So I don't fall down," the boy explained, pointing at the misty void below. "But I wouldn't fall. Unchain me, Uncle."

At this moment another voice cried: "Unchain me, Uncle, not him; he'll fall." Franciszek turned. A few steps away a little girl was chained, and then another girl; farther on, two little boys were playing, unconcerned with those around them; they had a pile of colored blocks in front of them.

"Where is your mother?"

"She went to work," said the first little boy. "What else could she do with us?" he added defensively. "Otherwise we'd be left alone in the room. This way we can play, at least." He picked up pieces of brick and began to throw them at the other children, who dodged the missiles, pressing their heads to the banister, squealing and melodiously clanking their chains. The girl's chain was decorated with ribbons. She held a doll whose head was attached to the banister with a chromium watch chain.

Franciszek was silent for a minute, then bent beside the little boy. He rummaged in his pockets, trying to find something to give him, but he found only his comb, mirror, and papers. He said: "You'll have to wait for Mama."

The boy twisted his mouth angrily. "I do, do I?" he said, jumping up like a monkey and rattling his chain. "Unchain me, Uncle. I've been here long enough. Or else, tell me a story. Do you know stories?"

"What story shall I tell you?" Franciszek pondered. The two boys at the end of the corridor started a fight, rolling furiously on the floor and getting entangled in their chains.

The boy said to Franciszek, "Tell me what you see down there." He pointed to the hole, and Franciszek leaned over, staring into the darkness till his eyes smarted. There was nothing unusual in the street; in fact there was scarcely anything to be seen. A drunk went by, then two drunks, then three drunks, one of them holding his hat in his hand; then a mother with a child, and an old man pushing a cart loaded with coal; there were drunken footsteps and sounds of laughter answered by cries of rage; and all that attracted the eye was the glow of the neon sign, which seemed to out-last the light of the stars.

"What do you see, Uncle?" the boy repeated, tugging Franciszek's trousers.

"The city," Franciszek said. "The city. Brightly lighted white houses, people coming home from work, laughing; now I see some boys running after a ball; and there's a little girl who just stumbled over her jump rope. Neon signs. And lights, lights, lights . . ." He stopped, and then asked the boy: "Where does the artist live here?"

"The one that makes statues of the little grandfather?"

"The little grandfather?"

"The little grandfather with the mustache. Is that the one you mean?"

"Yes."

"The door at the end," the boy said. And when Franciszek walked off, he cried after him, "Uncle, come and see me again."

"I'll come," Franciszek said. As he looked at the faintly gleaming bell, he thought: "Another door. What have I come for? What do I expect? You, behind this door, you can't be different. And that's what I have come for. I didn't leave my room: I'll just be looking into a mirror. I'll open the door to myself. Shall I turn back?" But he knocked. A man in a dressing gown examined him carefully before showing him in. They crossed a dark entrance hall, and suddenly Franciszek found himself within a circle of light—a bright, incredibly glaring light, which the other used in his workshop. He closed his eyes and mechanically sat down on the chair that had been pushed over to him. Only after a long while did he reopen his eyes, slowly, with an effort, like a man preparing to feel pain.

"Coffee?" asked the painter.

"No, thanks."

"Tea?"

He shook his head. "Don't put yourself out—" he began, but the painter interrupted him.

"Stop," he said, raising his hand imperiously. "Every word delays our joy. These are mere formalities: I have no tea or coffee anyway. We'll drink vodka."

He left him in the painful glare, and after a while came back with a bottle and two glasses, which he put on the rough, paint-spattered table. He filled the glasses, humming a tune.

"To your health," he said, raising his glass.

"Your health," Franciszek said after him.

They drank. The painter refilled their glasses.

"To the underground," Franciszek said, raising his glass. But the painter put his down. "Why the underground?" he asked. "What underground? Why the underground, rather, for instance, than the eternal beauty of pretty girls?"

"To the underground," Franciszek repeated. "We were both in the underground."

"When?"

"I don't know when," he said closing his eyes; the weird glare was splitting his head. "Can glare have a color?" he thought. "It can. White. This is a white glare." He said, "During the war."

"Right," the painter said, staring at the bottom of his glass. "Absolutely right. We are heroes, aren't we? I forgot. I beg your pardon. Your health."

They clinked glasses.

"And yours."

They lighted cigarettes; they looked at each other, incredulous, finding nothing, striking no spark; outside, the city whirred insistently, cats screamed in the corridor; boys' voices chanted monotonously, "Unchain me, Uncle; unchain me, Auntie . . ." Suddenly their eyes met; and both smiled with relief.

"Now I remember," the painter said. "You're Skinny, aren't you?"

"Yes," Franciszek said, "and you're Historian."

"They've certainly made a mess of us," the painter said, smiling happily. "It's just plain shit, isn't it?"

"Shit," Franciszek said. "What have I come here for, for God's sake? I wanted only one thing—I wanted you to be different from me, to think differently, speak differently, I don't know; maybe I wanted to say something, and I wanted you to answer by spitting in my face . . ." Turning his empty glass in his hands, he said: "It might be a good thing to agree once and for all that the whole thing is senseless. In fact I can go now."

"Have you joined the secret police yet?"

"No. And you?"

"I haven't either."

"So I can go now."

"As a matter of fact you can," the painter said. "You can go and you can give up the idea of going anywhere else, no matter where. You won't hear anything different. But you can try to fool yourself. You may succeed. That's what everyone else is doing."

Franciszek looked about the studio and suddenly realized why there was such a glare. Everywhere busts of the Great Teacher were piled up; the snow-white plaster sharply reflected the light of the bulbs; identical mustachioed faces stared with dead eyes from every wall.

"Christ," Franciszek stammered. "Why have you got so many of them?"

"Commissions," the painter said. "Easy, clean work:

plaster, water, a mold. They sell like hot cakes. I have a cus-
tomer who runs a clandestine shooting gallery on the out-
skirts. We Poles always like to protest . . ." He hummed a tune,
then said, sighing: "At first I modeled only the Prime Minister
and St. Francis of Assisi. Easy work; they're both bald. But no
one can compete with *him*." He picked up a cast. "Socialism's
pin-up Number One. Want one for a souvenir?"

Franciszek did not answer. He sat motionless, his head
between his fists. From every corner of the studio a dead face
stared at him. Someone walked by in the corridor, accompa-
nied by an imploring chorus of "Unchain me, Auntie."

"Do they always cry like that?"

"No," said the painter. "Only up to a certain age. Then they
can move about safely."

"We called you Historian," said Franciszek. "I remember
that after the war you were going to paint everything we experienced—the woods, the fights, man triumphing over fear,
and fear triumphing over man. Life and death. Even then you
were making sketches."

"I don't give a damn about what happened then," the
painter said. "I threw out my sketches. I don't want to talk
about it. Everything's all right the way it is. So far as I'm concerned, it can go on like this forever. I understand too much
to be interested in anything."

"It's funny," Franciszek said. "Man always dreamed of
one thing—knowledge. That was the meaning of his eternal
struggle. He dreamed of only one thing—to understand his
times, his purpose, his place, his meaning, and his moment
in eternity. And now that he has come closest to this understanding, knowledge is his main enemy. It's better not to understand—knowledge is a disease."

"No," the painter said. "It's death. It's worse than death.

It's an encore piece, an encore to something that didn't exist, that couldn't be taken seriously." He waved the bottle joyfully. "How about a drink?"

"Gladly," Franciszek said. Again he turned the glass in his fingers and blinked; the faces on the walls were hurting his eyes. He looked at the bit of vodka running back and forth on the flat bottom of the glass. "That's how the whole thing began," he said. "Just like that."

"How what began?"

"My case. My downfall."

"Just recently?"

"Yes. But that's beside the point. You aren't an imbecile either, and yet you're alive."

"I just don't pay any attention to it," the painter said, raising his glass. "Your health."

"And yours." He drank and put down his glass. "Do you know what?" he said. "A few days ago I went to see Birch."

"Birch?" the painter asked, surprised. He smiled. "So far as I know he is now called Rocking Horse."

"Rocking Horse?"

"Yes. He specializes in psychological questioning. It begins like this: he climbs on his desk and jumps on the prisoner's ribs. That's how he got the nickname. He hits the genitals with the butt of his gun. He organizes orgies and police courts. A real jokester. People shit with fear at the mere mention of his name."

"Nice," Franciszek said. He smiled. "He told me such moving stories."

"That's right," the painter said. "There were stories all right. About that son of his, am I right?"

"About his son, yes."

"Well, that's fine. Another drink?"

"Sure."

They drank. Again the children in the corridor responded to footsteps with an "Unchain me, Auntie." Then a cat screamed. Then a dog growled. Then came the sound of heavy footsteps, and the children intoned: "Uncle, unchain us, just for a minute . . ."

"How about coffee?" the painter asked after a while.

"No, thanks."

"Tea?"

"Don't trouble yourself . . ."

"No trouble at all," the painter said. "All I have is vodka. For the last five years I haven't taken a drop of water. My questions are just a way of talking; you have got to get used to them. Excuse me." He rose, shuffled over to a corner of his enormous studio, and came back with a new bottle. The little boys outside, the cats, and the dog screamed in unison. The painter set the glasses down side by side and filled them as though they were measuring cups—not a millimeter's difference between them.

"To the trees," the painter said.

Franciszek opened his eyes; for a moment he did not understand the glare or the other's words. "To what trees?" he said.

"The woods, the underground. We fought together in the woods," the painter explained impatiently. "We're heroes, aren't we? We made a revolution; we were partisan fighters. Have you forgotten?"

"No."

"Well?"

"Does all that count?"

"Alas. Idiots and criminals are given no credit. Nor heroes. Do you know who we are?"

"No. And you?"

"I don't either. But I'm not interested any more. I'm a corpse. Like you. Like Communism. And that's all. I often think of Hitler. What did he accomplish, when all is said and done? Yes, he went to a great deal of trouble; but in the end, what did he achieve? He murdered more people than any decent man murders in his mind. He tried to be consistent, and he succeeded as far as his stupidity would let him. But in the end he failed like every other Savior. That's all. The Great Teacher accomplished far greater things. He built a grave-yard. From now on, future generations will be born and live in graveyards, Apparently people march toward life, toward the sun, through graves. I stick it all up my ass . . ." He sud-denly leaned toward Franciszek and seized his wrist with ter-rible strength. "Tell me," he hissed, "are you with the secret police, or not?"

"Not yet. And you?"

"Not yet, either. I'll tell you myself when I am."

"So there's nothing to be done?"

"Nothing. Communism ought to be saved from Com-munism. But people won't go without an idea, never. It would be easy to die if this were mankind's last great myth. To die, to commit the greatest crimes, so that people should never again believe in any sun. But it's no use. After a while some new madman will come along; he'll get hold of an icon and run through the city carrying it . . ." He gave a short laugh. "If I were born again," he said, "and if I wanted to take revenge on people, I'd create a new ideology for them. To lead crowds to the sunny days of the future—that's the biggest joke of all."

"That's how it's got to be," Franciszek said. "No man can endure knowledge. He's got no right to ask for it. It's mythol-ogy, not knowledge, that holds societies together."

"Well, then," the painter said, "go ahead, create a new idea. Any Christ will be useful to mankind. Up to the point of crucifixion, everything is fine, speaking of great ideas. But resurrection is madness. It's too bad, but I keep repeating myself. Besides, today Christ would be given the psychological treatment. That's a sign of progress. I drink to the crumbling Cross. Hurrah."

"Hurrah."

Their heads were spinning now, and the glare became still more intense. They were in the middle of the city; in the heart of the dying night with its dirty puddles. They were surrounded and nailed by the dead stares of dozens of eyes. Franciszek suddenly had the feeling that he had never seen any face but this one rigidly smiling face, and that he, the painter, Elzbieta, the boy squealing in the corridor, and all people struggling on this earth looked exactly alike. That was how man looked, and his problem, too—the special problem of this unfortunate creature, the question of loyalty and conscience which God, Satan, or Nature foisted upon man to make his life even more precarious, anxious, and difficult than it would normally be.

"No," he said, "that's not the worst of it. If I go on living, it means that I accept all this, and I have no right to squawk. A man can live through any hell, survive any tyranny, get out of any swamp and any oppression, if he has at least a crumb of certainty, or at least hope, that there is somewhere another man who walks and breathes like him; who suffers, seeks, or fights like him, preserving his purity. Among us, none can have this hope. Here, among us, the heart of the world has died. Here the great myth of the poor gave up the ghost. Not somewhere else, but here; in this place, toward which the eyes of all the unfortunate and oppressed are turned. Here died the world's faith. All the words. All the ideas. All the dreams of man's emancipation. You are right: this is a graveyard. This is the worst. Where can we find strength?"

"What do you mean, where?" the painter said. "In our certainty that there will always be idiots. That's the worst of it. Are you looking for comfort?"

"Yes," Franciszek said. "I want to be comforted."

"There is no comfort," the painter said. "If there was any-thing more idiotic, piggish, and useless than human life, it might be a comfort. Unfortunately, no such thing has ever been discovered, but mankind is waiting for its great day. For the time being they have invented eternity, the one with a dung heap of rotten corpses. Try to get there if it amuses you. After all, we're all going there, and in the face of eternity man always assumes the position of somebody who has been kicked in the ass. Such is the meaning of glory and fame."

"And if," Franciszek said, "if I could find at least one man from among our companions who thinks differently?" He looked at the painter with burning eyes. "And Jerzy?" he asked gently.

"What about Jerzy?"

"Does he think the same way?"

Both fell silent; and suddenly the stillness was solemn. Outside the window, invisible, the city hummed in the dark-ness, like an enormous insect. Shadows and lights darted across the ceiling; the stove creaked monotonously; and both of them, Franciszek and the painter, suddenly felt the presence of something great, something that was true and solemn; it was as though Eternity had come closer with its indifferent face that no one has ever fully seen.

"Yes," the painter said at last. He bent his enormous head, staring at his paint-corroded hands that lay folded on his

knees. "Maybe he is different. Men like him do not perish."
He raised his head abruptly. "Listen," he said. "Go to see him.
Go right away; don't wait. He alone can help you. He was the
best of us. The purest. He's the only man you can trust. Go."

"Come with me," Franciszek said. He looked at him
searchingly, and saw a sudden gleam in the other's eyes, brief
as the beat of a wing. Then again his eyes were like those of
a statue.

"No," he said, "I'll never go ..." He pointed to the gleaming busts. "I have commissions; I must work. This is the only
hope."

"What is?"

"To wait," the painter said, "to wait in the hope that I'll live
to see the day when people smash my masterpieces openly.
That's the only thing. Adieu."

"What shall I tell him about you?"

"About me? A message from me?"

"Well?"

"That's easy, Franciszek," the painter said. "That's easy. The
same as about all of us. That I am dead. Goodbye. Come back
someday for a cup of tea."

Franciszek left. Again he walked down the dark corridor; cats and dogs were squealing; he tottered in the dust and
darkness, pulling the cuffs of his trousers out of the grasp of
one child's hands after another's.

# XV

"IS TODAY SUNDAY?" FRANCISZEK ASKED.

"No," Elzbieta said, "only Friday."

He put down his shaving things, and turned away from the mirror. "Then why don't you go to your courses?" he asked.

She was silent, her head bowed. Her eyes were swollen, ringed with blue circles; in the last few days her face had become strangely small and gray, and the corners of her mouth drooped. He came over to her and stood helpless, waiting for her to give some sign of life; but she sat motionless, with a hostile expression she had never shown before. "Well," he said.

"I have no courses today," she said. "Neither today nor tomorrow . . ."

She tried to rise, but he held her down. "My little girl," he began.

She pushed him away with unexpected force, as though this pet name were particularly repulsive to her. "Go away."

"What happened?"

"Nothing happened," she cried. "Why should anything happen? Just leave me alone."

He went out without breakfast, hungry, badly shaved. Still no sign of spring; for weeks now it had been raining and

sleeting; for weeks the city had been drenched. The dampness was of a special kind, dirty, loathsome, unbearable, for
the branches of the anemic trees remained hard and dry. The
fat eye of the sun blinked in the gray sky—its presence was
pointless and only made one angry. "What's the matter with
this spring?" he thought, as he walked along staring at the
sky. "Have I ever lived through such a spring?" At the corner he saw a telephone booth; there was no one behind the
glass door. He entered, dialed, and once again heard the same
woman's voice.

"May I speak to Jerzy?"

"Who is it?"

"Kowalski," he said. "Franciszek Kowalski ... So Jerzy is
back?"

"Please hold on a minute," the woman said, and put down
the receiver. He waited with a pounding heart. Finally she
came back. "Jerzy is a bit unwell," she said. "Can you come
this afternoon?"

"Yes," he said, "of course. I'll come straight from work.
Goodbye."

"Hullo," the woman said in a hushed voice. "Just a second.
Can you hear me? Jerzy is a bit unwell. Jerzy doesn't feel well.
Please remember that. You do understand me, don't you?"

"Yes," he said; "it's no wonder in this weather. Goodbye.
I'll come right after work."

He hung up and walked out; again he hurried to work
through crowds of peevish people cursing one another, trampling on one another's toes. Someone loudly threatened to
report the conductor, who barked back from the other end
of the car, "You make it hard for people to work." "Oh, stick
it up ..." "Go f— yourself." Franciszek looked at the damp
gray walls passing outside the window, and thought, "Spring,

spring ..." "You're a tramp!" a fat man shouted, waving his
brief case over the passengers' heads. "Do you hear me?"
"And you, you're a Soviet scientist." The passengers crowd-
ing the platform squealed timidly with joy. "What's the matter?" a brisk, familiar voice said suddenly. "Someone here
that doesn't like it? Tell the truth; do you like it or don't you?"
"Here you are," Franciszek thought. "Here you are; I've been
waiting for your voice. You had to come ..." The car stopped;
Franciszek stood on his toes, and looked out; the policeman
was marching a group of arrested men down the street.

    Several hours later the siren howled; he could hardly wait
for its second howl, the one that marked the end of the working day; and when finally he heard it he was the first to run
across the courtyard, deafened by the sound of his own heart,
which did not stop pounding even when he stood in front of
Jerzy's door. He stood with his arms dangling, without the
strength to ring the bell. He was silent, paralyzed before the
last door of this city. He was silent even when the lady of
the house helped him with his overcoat, and he heard nothing
of what she said to him as she led him through the entrance
hall—it was strangely long, somehow old-fashioned, dark,
full of cabinets, chests, and infernal rugs that made walking hazardous. At last he entered the living room. "Jerzy," he
said, "Jerzy."

    Tears veiled his eyes, and he could not see the man stand-
ing before him, saying something in a loud voice and vigorously shaking his hand. He was not ashamed of his tears
and his stammering. He knew that he had finally reached
some sort of destination, that he had come to the end of
his wanderings, and that he had achieved peace; he did not
know what kind of peace, but it was peace. At last he recovered himself, and looked at the other. Before him stood a

miserable skeleton with sunken cheeks and completely lusterless eyes, in a suit pitifully too large for him—his thin arms
protruded ludicrously from the baggy sleeves. This was Jerzy;
nothing else was important. They sat down, stammering and
patting each other's knees.

"Well, Franciszek," Jerzy said. "What's new with you?"

"Jerzy," Franciszek said. "This won't sound clever. I don't
even know how to say it. I only know my reason for coming
here. Give me again what you gave me once before. Once, in
the woods. Once when I was near the end."

"What is it, Skinny?"

They smiled at each other, looking straight into each
other's eyes. Franciszek started: the skeleton sitting before
him had smiled, uncovering the toothless gums of an old
man.

"What is it, Skinny?" the former commander repeated.

"Faith. Faith in something, anything. If only in the fact
that you haven't changed."

"I have not changed," Jerzy said. He said it too quickly.
Franciszek saw fear in his eyes. Or perhaps it was not fear; but
whatever it was, it was not faith. He smiled, and said, "You
have changed."

"Faith," Jerzy said. He rose and approached Franciszek,
and put his emaciated hands on his shoulders. "Where is your
faith, Franciszek?" he said, looking at him sternly. "Where is
your faith? Don't you see anything?"

"I do see," Franciszek said. "Wherever I turn I see things
against which a man must stand up and fight. Is there still any
fight and any meaning left?"

"I see something else," Jerzy said, staring into a corner of
the room. Then he began to speak very fast, choking on his
own saliva. "I see emancipated man. Man who was victorious

over himself and renounced himself. There is no other victory. This is the ultimate purpose: not to think of yourself in
victory. Every conqueror must first kill himself . . ." He turned
away, and Franciszek saw with horror that tears were rolling
down his sunken cheeks. "Man," Jerzy stammered, raising his
fists above his head, and shaking them helplessly. "Man, man
was everywhere. At the ends of the earth, on mountain peaks,
and in the ocean depths. He invented the multiplication table
and the atomic pile, motion pictures and radio, the steam
engine and penicillin; he was in concentration camps and in
crematoria, and yet he lives, is reborn, multiplies. There is life
for you; there is victory. And you ask about faith. Where is
your faith, you brute?" he cried wildly. "Where is your faith? I
haven't changed; I was, I am, and I will be as you have known
me to be. Once again you don't trust me. Once again you are
sending your spies to my house." He stretched out his arm
in a theatrical gesture and pointed to the door. "Get out!" he
cried. "I don't want to see you. I don't want to see anyone. I
have done what you asked of me, and now let me alone . . ."
He stood silent as a statue for a while, and then threw himself
on his knees before Franciszek: "Forgive me," he whispered.
"I know a great deal. I know everything; I can be useful. I
know what people think—all of them, all, all. We'll get into
every thought, every action, every corner of the human brain,
even where thoughts are born. But that's not true," he cried.
"There are no bad thoughts. It's possible to think only the way
we want, or not to think at all. Other thoughts are useless.
We've had enough thoughts that lead to nothing. Now we
must conquer." He kissed Franciszek's hand with his slobber-
ing mouth. "We'll conquer," he squeaked. "We'll conquer everything. Only some things must be changed. We'll conquer
even dreams; stupid dreams can also lead to deviations. We

must conquer dreams!" he shouted with ferocious strength, pinching Franciszek's arms with his bony fingers. "That will be our task. And now, sing."

He sang shrilly, staring at Franciszek with murky eyes: "This is the fi-nal . . ."

His arms were twitching convulsively; tears seeped through his fingers with which he had covered his decrepit face. He looked hideous; his gray head shook pitifully on his thin red neck. Franciszek sat rigid and half unconscious from horror. Someone jerked his arm.

"Go now," the woman said. "Please, go now."

He silently put on his overcoat.

"Didn't you know?" she said.

"I didn't."

"He was arrested," she said. "They kept him two years. They questioned him in their own way. He won't tell me, even me, how it was. Every time a visitor comes, he thinks it's someone sent from there. That's why he has those terrible fits . . ." She came close to him. "You really didn't know that he is . . ." She hesitated.

"He's not the only one," Franciszek said. "Everybody is. Please, never mention me to him."

"He doesn't understand anyhow," she said.

"So much the better for him. Good night."

# XVI

HE WAS ABOUT TO CLIMB THE STAIRS IN HIS apartment house, when someone called after him, "Hey, Citizen Kowalski."

He stopped. It was the janitor, a miserable-looking fellow in a shoddy blue jacket. They stood silent, looking at each other; the janitor's expression betrayed embarrassment. A few floors up on the staircase, two men were carrying something large and heavy; they were noisy, and one kept crying to the other, "Stefan, take it sideways . . ."

"What's the matter?" Franciszek asked. And when the other did not answer, he repeated: "What's the matter, Citizen Superintendent?"

The janitor stared a few more moments with doglike eyes, then turned on his heel and went back to his room. Franciszek shrugged and began to climb the stairs. He was surprised: despite the late hour tenants were standing outside almost every door—women in wrappers, men with their suspenders hanging, some old men, some students; even a drunken soldier had strayed in from somewhere. All of them were whispering and gesticulating feverishly; their eyes betrayed great excitement; but when Franciszek passed them, the whispers ceased, and the people retreated into the shadows. On one landing, an elderly man was trying to open his window; he tugged vainly at the brass handle, repeating angrily, "The young, the young ..." "Where are these people from?" Franciszek thought sleepily. "Why are there so many people in this house?" He kept bumping into them, forcing his way through them: he lived on one of the upper floors, and walked very slowly; he was tired, so tired that he became aware of the sweetish smell of gas only when he reached the dark corridor leading to his door—his door which was bashed in and hung crookedly on one hinge. Out stepped a man in a rubber apron, with a mask on his face.

Elzbieta was lying on her side, curled and strangely twisted like a bird that has been shot down. The veins in both her arms had been opened in two places, below the elbows and above the wrists. The doctor had finished packing his case; two male nurses stood beside him, holding their masks. The blood had already coagulated and hardened; the wind blew through the smashed window, tearing at the curtain. The doctor looked at Franciszek and said, "About two hours ago."

Franciszek nodded. With firm steps he walked to the table, took the envelope and opened it. "Forgive me," she had written, "but this is the best thing for me to do. You were expelled from the party and Mikołaj left home; Mikołaj left home and I was expelled from the university—children of people expelled from the party have no right to study. I broke with Roman because of a statement he voluntarily made and signed—that it was wrong of him to live with the daughter of a man like you. I don't want this chain of events to reach my child, and it is too late to prevent it in any other way. The money is in the cupboard. The laundress will come on Tuesday. Farewell."

The doctor asked: "Will you come with us to the morgue?"

"To the morgue?" Franciszek said with surprise. "No."

"Can I do anything for you? Shall I give you a sedative?"

"Oh," said Franciszek, annoyed, "leave me alone ..." He walked to the bed and looked at Elzbieta's rigid face. The bed stood near the window, and whenever the wind lifted the curtain a red glow flickered in Elzbieta's milky eyes. "Where does this light come from?" Franciszek murmured. He turned to the doctor. "Are you sure?"

"Try to get some sleep," the doctor said. "Tomorrow you'll have to attend to the formalities."

"All right," Franciszek said. "But tomorrow."

"Of course."

One of the nurses said, "We had to smash a window," and waved the mask he was holding. The other said: "There is a glazier across the street. I live there. Shall I write down his address for you?"

"Thanks," Franciszek said. "I'll remember. Across the street, you said?"

"Yes."

They walked out, bending under the burden; the doctor smiled stupidly and walked out too; for another moment Franciszek heard their footsteps on the stairs, and the murmur of voices; then the draft slammed the door shut. He raised the collar of his overcoat and went to the window; another gust of wind lifted the curtain, and he understood where the red glow in Elzbieta's eyes had come from. The neon sign was blazing triumphantly, with assurance; even the missing letters had been replaced. In the dirty starless sky, above the damp mass of the city, the enormous letters quivered. This time he read them carefully, one by one, like something hitherto unnoticed and now discovered for the first time.

# XVII

COLD WEATHER AND RAIN HAD LONG TORMENTED the city; and the fact that May Day fell on the first cheerful and warm day made it a doubly joyful occasion—as was duly pointed out by the radio and the press. From the early hours of the morning the streets had been filled with people, animated and wearing their May Day best; parades were forming on the large squares; a thousand huge loudspeakers set up for the purpose roared sprightly marches and songs. In the motley crowd regional costumes stood out brightly—the mountaineers' caps with their black tassels, the open collars and fancy jackets of the miners whose joyous faces were concealed behind the colored glass of their masks. The wind flapped the banners and wreaths, and the sun had had time to put a flush on the faces of those who had been out since morning—it was a truly beautiful day. Finally, at noon, solemnly announced by the city clocks, the procession set out.

A slightly drunk little man in a shabby suit stood near the curb of a crowded sidewalk. He stared intensely at the briskly marching people, and under his breath read off the inscriptions on the banners: "Our answer to the atom bomb—we build new houses," "Man is our supreme good," "The working class leads the people," and so on. The little drunk rubbed his hands and laughed softly, but happily; he stood on tiptoe,

thrust his head under the arms of people in front of him, and
when he saw, among the marching throngs, the groups of
workers from the "For a Better Tomorrow" automobile repair
factory, he began to clap so loudly that everybody beamed
and nodded in approval. Indeed the group of the workers
from "For a Better Tomorrow" presented an impressive ap-
pearance: they were carrying a huge model of a car, and all of
them wore identical blue overalls; one of the marchers even
led a magnificent Airedale terrier on a leash: the beautiful
dog had a red cockade tied to its head, and an artistically
wrought muzzle on its thoroughbred snout. The little man,
seized by euphoria, clapped so vigorously and enthusiasti-
cally that at one point he tottered with exhaustion, falling
against the man standing behind him, who calmly but firmly
restored the drunk to his former position by nudging him
with his knee.

"Hey," the little man said indignantly, "stop shoving."

"What's the matter?" the man behind him said in a brisk
voice. "Maybe you don't like it? Now tell the truth, do you like
it or don't you?"

The little man turned as though struck by an electric current. He saw a sturdy, handsome policeman in dress uniform.
The buckle of his belt, the metal edge of his visor, his clasps,
the brass butt of his gun, the new leather belt and boots—
all these things gleamed so brightly in the spring sun that it
hurt the eyes to look at them. The little man smiled happily.
"So you're here too?" he said.

"Of course," the policeman replied, and once again gently pushed the little man with his knee. This time, the little
man moved forward without protesting, and even tipped his
greasy hat.

"Yes," the little man said, "yes . . ." Happily rubbing his

dirty hands, he repeated: "Yes, yes ... You remember me, of course?"

The policeman glanced at him and gave a superior smile. "Disturbance of the peace at night," he said. "I took you to the police station."

"Yes, yes," the little man said eagerly, "it was you. You yourself—I mean you in person. Because there was another policeman with you, right?" He staggered again, but another push righted him and restored his dignity.

"Right," the policeman said. "What of it? Maybe you don't ..."

The little man interrupted him with a wave of his hand. "Everything's perfect," he said. "It seems I said a lot of things that time. Otherwise I would've had to march with these people here. As it is, I'm standing comfortably, as you see. All the more so because this is a fairly long parade: those in front are executed by firing squads, and those in back see nothing and sing."

"Well, I'll be d—"

"Sure," the little man said. "Don't you remember? I told you then, my dear man: the crimes, the distortions, the ideology replaced with totalitarianism, all this does no harm to anyone. Man's drama cannot be handed down to posterity: while one generation matures and accumulates experience, history produces a new generation of carefree folk who willingly join the ranks. You don't have to worry: you'll have a job to the end of your days. Just as I told you then."

"When?" the policeman said. "When?"

The little man wagged his finger in his face and began to giggle. "You're a joker, a joker." He burst out laughing. "And as for me, you know," he said, "I got into some trouble because of that."

"Because of what?"

The little man grew suddenly angry. "What do you mean, because of what?" he cried. Once again the other's knee put him in his place. "Because of what I said then. I said all that to you and the others in the police station. What do you think? This parade, these happy faces? It's all exactly as it should be, and I believe that everything's perfect, everything—just as I said. Every tyranny ends more or less like a woman's beauty: the more magnificent the façade, the more rotten the core; the prettier the dress, the filthier the body; the more talk about strength and loyalty, the more terrorism and the weaker the rulers. Whores and tyrants end the same way—can't you understand even the simplest things? But here everything fits like a jigsaw puzzle. What do you want, what do you lack? Hope? You have hope: the knowledge that thousands of others are as pushed around and despised as I am, that those who were born before us were just as pushed around and despised, and that those who will be born after us will be treated the same way. Doesn't all this make you happy? How many times must I tell you, ha?"

"Wait a minute," the policeman said, rubbing his forehead. "When did you tell me that?"

"Then," the little man said, "it was then that I told you all that. But then or now, sooner or later, what's the difference? You'll always find someone who understands too much and who will have to die for it. And even if he doesn't understand, it will always be necessary to find someone or other, to denounce him and accuse him for nothing, and to no purpose; a man who will be tracked down and tormented, and who in the end will be caught and put to death; who will be ordered to sing a hymn in honor of his killers; and this will have to be done if only to stop other members of society from some day conceiving the idea that they can decide the fate of others. That's how it should be; and, damn it all, why should any of this surprise you? What is man, after all is said and done, man with all his sufferings, aspirations, loves? An eternal absurdity in the infinite. To save man from realizing this, it will always be necessary to find some Franciszek or other."

The policeman's healthy face displayed boundless despair. "What Franciszek?" he asked, wiping the sweat off his forehead. "Saint Francis of Assisi?"

"No," the little man said, stamping his foot angrily. "I've always told you, there aren't any heroes or saints; there's only necessity which forever and ever squeezes what is required out of man. Why a saint? Kowalski is enough. With every Kowalski one can do what is necessary, one way or another, if circumstances so require."

"Mister," said the policeman. "Who did you say all this to? Please tell me, or I'll go into this passageway and shoot myself. Tell me, tell me," he cried tearfully. "I can't stand not knowing."

"To you," the little man said vengefully. "To you and the others. Then, in the police station."

"You're the biggest fool I've ever met," the policeman said, his face expressing enormous relief. "You didn't say a thing, and that's why we let you go. You were calm and polite; in fact all of us took a liking to you. We saw you were a party man, soft-spoken, quiet—so we just put a bit of a scare into you and let you go in the morning. Our chief treats everybody like that, even if it's some lousy virgin straight from her first communion. The moment somebody turns up at the police station, we've got to scare him, no matter who he is. We scared you for your own good, so that next time you'd stay sober, and wouldn't lose your job, and your papers wouldn't be taken away from you. Understand?"

Franciszek was silent. In the end he said, "So I didn't say anything."

"Not a word. I mean, pee-pee, and so on. But nothing bad."

"And I'm innocent."

"Sure. We let you go, and the statement went in the wastebasket, and that was that. We do our best to help people. Everybody knows the whole thing doesn't amount to a hill of beans, and you didn't have to explain anything to anyone; if you'd tried to explain, you'd have been punched in the jaw, and sent to solitary. Go home and pull yourself together."

"There are no homes any more," Franciszek said after a while. "There are only graveyards ... So everybody lied. What a joke! You, the secretary, and Jerzy. But now it's not important any more: the truth has turned out to be even stupider than I thought ..."

"Come, come," the policeman said. "Maybe you don't like it?"

They measured each other.

"No," Franciszek said.

"No?"

"No."

"You really don't?"

"I really don't."

Both stood up straight; and at once both felt enormous relief; they stood motionless, looking at each other—pure and calm; calm as always when something important is about to begin.

"Let's go," the policeman said.

"Let's go," Franciszek said.

They pushed into the crowd; the joyous throng separated them for a moment. Franciszek looked about him; he saw the gleam of the policeman's cap a little way off. He forced a passage toward him. "Give me your hand!" he cried. "Give me your hand, or I'll lose my way again!"

# THE NEVERSINK LIBRARY

# THE NEVERSINK LIBRARY

# THE NEVERSINK LIBRARY

**THE POLYGLOTS**
by William Gerhardie

978-1-61219-188-1
$17.00 / $17.00 CAN

**MY AUTOBIOGRAPHY**
by Charlie Chaplin

978-1-61219-192-8
$20.00 / $20.00 CAN

**WHERE THERE'S LOVE, THERE'S HATE**
by Adolfo Bioy Casares
and Silvina Ocampo

978-1-61219-150-8
$15.00 / $15.00 CAN

**THE DIFFICULTY OF BEING**
by Jean Cocteau

978-1-61219-290-1
$15.95 / $15.95 CAN

**THE OASIS**
by Mary McCarthy

978-1-61219-228-4
$15.00 / $15.00 CAN

**COLLEGE OF ONE**
by Sheilah Graham

978-1-61219-283-3
$15.95 / $15.95 CAN

**DEFINITELY MAYBE**
by Arkady and Boris Strugatsky

978-1-61219-281-9
$15.00 / $15.00 CAN

**GILGI**
by Irmgard Keun

978-1-61219-277-2
$16.00 / $16.00 CAN

**THE GRAVEYARD**
by Marek Hłasko

978-1-61219-294-9
$15.95 / $15.95 CAN

**REASONS OF STATE**
by Alejo Carpentier

978-1-61219-279-6
$16.00 / $16.00 CAN

**ZULEIKA DOBSON**
by Max Beerbohm

978-1-61219-292-5
$15.95 / $15.95 CAN